"The characters in [...] people novelists to [...] unworthy of our notice. In Martin Hyatt's compassionate hands they come fully to life in all their haunting despair."
—Jaime Manrique,
author of *Latin Moon in Manhattan*

"Martin Hyatt's narrative *tour de force* takes us deep into the unchronicled heart of rural working-class gay life in the Deep South. Hyatt is a merciless, merciful storyteller, showing us the people sacrificed to bigotry, and those who snatched themselves, scarred and beautiful, out of its murderous jaws."
—Minnie Bruce Pratt,
author of *S/He*

"Lyrical and anguished, this is a stunning first novel about the despair of addiction and the hope provided by love. The writing is so skillful it's hard to believe that this is a debut. Hallucinated scenes from the past enter into the dreamlike present to create a tapestry of pain and solace. If this is a gay novel it's unlike any other I've ever read."
—Edmund White,
author of *A Boy's Own Story*

A SCARECROW'S BIBLE

A SCARECROW'S BIBLE

MARTIN HYATT

suspect thoughts press
www.suspectthoughtspress.com

Author photograph by Worth Gurley
Cover image and design by Shane Luitjens/Torquere Creative
Book design by Greg Wharton/Suspect Thoughts Press

First Edition: February 2006
10 9 8 7 6 5 4 3 2 1

Library of Congress Cataloging-in-Publication Data

Hyatt, Martin.
  A scarecrow's bible / by Martin Hyatt.
      p. cm.
  ISBN-13: 978-0-9763411-4-7 (pbk.)
  ISBN-10: 0-9763411-4-X (pbk.)
  1. Vietnamese Conflict, 1961-1975--Veterans--Fiction. 2. Drug addicts--Fiction. 3. Gay men--Fiction. I. Title.

PS3608.Y36S28 2005
813'.6--dc22

                                                    2005027368

Suspect Thoughts Press
2215-R Market Street, #544
San Francisco, CA 94114-1612
www.suspectthoughtspress.com

For my mother, Maudine, and my father, Martin, for the books and the typewriters.

For James. For Christy, Lisa, the Ronnies. Aunt Juanita. Uncle Denman.

For anyone who has ever inspired me.

Thank you to Greg and Ian: innovators, visionaries.

Thank you to my students for keeping me going.

Thank you to the mentors and teachers who showed me the way: Edward Albee, Michael Cunningham, Abigail Thomas, Minnie Bruce Pratt, David Gates, Francine Prose, Darcey Steinke, Lynda Schor, Shelley Smith, Jan Donley, Jon Batdorff.

Thank you to Jackson Taylor of The New School University's MFA Program for not giving up on me. Thank you to Goddard College for helping me to find my voice.

Thank you to Massimo Porrati for ten years and for the love.

Thank you to Elizabeth Ojakian for listening.

Thank you to the artistic angels who keep me going: Anne Marie Rose, Erin Foley, Olivia Hayman, Jennifer Fink.

Thank you to my radio heroes who wrote my life without knowing it: Nanci Griffith, Steve Earle, Mary Chapin Carpenter, Lucinda Williams, Rosanne Cash, Courtney Love.

Thank you to the places I call home: New York City, California, New Orleans.

And finally, for everyone who struggles in anonymity one day at a time.

Death whistles and rings of muffled music cause this worshiped body to rise up, expand, and tremble like a ghost. Scarlet and black break out on the proud flesh. The very colors of life deepen, dance, and stand out from the vision in the yard... Our bones are reclothed with a new body of love...

— Rimbaud, "Being Beauteous"
from *The Illuminations*

1

October is the time of year when you most feel yourself being pushed over the edge. This is home. After dinner, you hear her in the kitchen, and you reach for the *TV Guide*. It is your life now, the end of the week, and you feel safe, and it is as though this is what the end of your life is supposed to be like. *60 Minutes* is on and the ticking clock reminds you of the century in which you live. The New Orleans Saints lost their game again today, a Sunday ritual of sorts.

You sit there, on the wheelbarrow-patterned couch that is missing a front leg. An encyclopedia bought from a traveling salesman years ago is placed beneath it, leveling it off, making it seem like nothing is missing at all. The *TV Guide*s are stacked high in the corner, as nobody in the house wants to throw them away. It's like they've been stacked for you to measure time, instead of remembering it. As they stand by the fish tank, you know one of these days they'll just come tumbling down, and that lonely goldfish in that oversized tank will finally see some action.

You stare at the pine clock shaped like Mississippi. This is how things are in this house around six o'clock. Gina is in the kitchen, baking an apple cobbler. Lula, your daughter, in her self-jailed room, is reading a mystery novel.

This gives you the opportunity to reach into your pocket and take some pills. Two Somas and two Valium, each for a different form of pain. Thank God for mad doctors with prescription pads.

You hear Gina turn on the dishwasher. Except for that and Mike Wallace's voice, the house trailer is quiet. Once in a while you hear Lula moving around her room. She's big like that. Too big to be your own daughter, but you love her as if she is actually your own. You wonder how she stood the summer in the heat. It's hard enough on thin people like you.

You reach behind you and stick out a hand, noticing how the hairs on it are growing less brown and more gray. You raise the window and feel the cool air blowing in from behind, then turn for a moment and stare out the window. Maybe this trailer isn't so bad after all, one of the biggest on the market. Between your job as a carpenter and Gina's small amount from working part-time at the Tastee-Freez, you have enough money to survive. But still, it is a trailer, and growing up you always promised yourself that you would not end up in the same type of place in which you grew up.

A police car with its lights on passes swiftly on the road outside, then turns away. You think about jumping out the window. It wouldn't be a far fall or anything. You would just find yourself outside for no reason, maybe even landing on your feet. Gina would think that it was time for another trip to the hospital, though. So instead you turn and stare at the room again, wishing Gina hadn't put out those cheap candles that are white and triangle-shaped and smell the way you hope that your clothes don't. You are wearing a T-shirt and khakis, that's all, and it's about fifty-five degrees outside with a slight wind. But you don't feel cold. Even though it was stifling over there, feeling cold is one of those things that you left behind in the jungle.

Gina walks into the room, and you look at the television. There are now lines running across it. As she comes closer to you, the television becomes fuzzy. She is standing there wearing a red-and-white-checkered apron, like the one she has always worn. The tinfoil on the antenna is just hanging there. You know that you can get up and fix it, but you don't really care what's on. The picture is all fuzzy now. Petulia must be the only place in America without cable television.

"What's going on?" you ask, knowing that nothing is.

"What are you thinking?" she asks.

"You can turn the TV off," you tell her. She seems to think about it for a moment, but leaves it on. Then she sits down beside you, smelling like decent perfume and Cajun spices. You wonder what you smell like to her. You think you smell like sweat, but hope that you smell like the basic white soap you showered with a little earlier.

You pull her close, because this is what husbands do. Her hair is still blonde. She is nearly fifty, and you know that she'll never go gray. Even when she was a cheerleader and you were both students at LSU, you knew she'd never grow old. Even with a few lines in her face, she still seems like she will live forever. And while you want her to go on living, you wonder if time has been as kind to you. During the first ten years of your marriage, she kept telling you that you looked like Paul Newman. You should have believed her then, because even though mirrors are not part of your daily life, you know your days of being handsome are behind you. Drinking and confusion have stolen your youth, while calmness has preserved hers. Sometimes you want to ask her what you look like, but you know what an honest person she is and you refrain.

"It's freezing in here," she says. Lately, the way she pulls away from you is like she never loved you. Maybe she's having an affair. You can't blame her.

She shuts the window.

"I have to go to bed," she says. "I just wanted to tell you that there is a cobbler on the stove, if you want some."

The television is beyond fuzzy and strangely lined now. It almost looks like gray grass. "Thanks," you say, kissing her on the cheek, knowing that a kiss on the lips would be a lie.

"Maybe Lula will want some. I'm worried about her.

She's always in that room reading. Maybe it's a phase."

"She's twenty-two, too old for phases." You say this, knowing personally that this is not true.

"Even her little friends at the community college don't come around anymore. Fine with me, though. Half of them were queer as a three-dollar bill, I think."

"Why do you think that?"

"You could tell, by the way they acted and everything. Like the way I'd walk in on them dancing and all of them sitting real close. The way their voices were so high and soft, like they were suppose to be in the women's choir or something. You know the type." She is staring at you intensely, obviously waiting for you to say something, but you have nothing to say, so you wait for her to continue. "But I guess it was better for her to have them around than nobody at all."

"I guess so." It's getting hot again.

"You know what I heard? That some of them even moved to the French Quarter."

"Imagine that," you say, actually imagining it.

You feel her staring at you, waiting for a response you refuse to give her, so she changes the subject. "Do you like the way that plant is growing?" she asks, referring to that giant green thing her mother brought for the two of you last year. You've heard her, but you don't respond.

You haven't been to New Orleans enough. And when you were there, you were always on edge. As though Gina was going to walk into that pub on the corner of Bourbon and St. Anne to remind you of who you said you were. That old bar, walled with open windowed doors that stayed open, was where you would spend all day drinking Midori Sours and watching Tennessee Williams characters walking by in the rain.

"Gary?"

New Orleans for you was like a nightclub in the

streets. A place where things could not only happen to you, but where they were supposed to.

"What?"

"The plant. Do you see how big it's getting? Remember when Mama give it to us last year before the holiday? It was nothing but a tiny thing."

In New Orleans, up on a balcony, on Bourbon Street, someone took your dick slowly into his mouth and sucked gently. He was so much younger. That's all you remember, then you ran away. Like the rest of your memories, this one ends without an end. But still, you do recall, standing against a wrought-iron fence, feeling him welcoming you into his mouth like it was a church where everyone prayed the same prayer. Before it was over, before the Amen, you ran away. Blackness had set in.

"I hate it," you finally say, more loudly than you expected. "I hate that big plant." It is a tall green palmy thing standing beside a bookcase full of Harold Robbins and Jackie Collins novels. "It's too big. It's too, too big..." The pills have finally kicked in. You know you've gone too far. She really loves that tree. So you out to reach for her; you say, "But if you like it..."

But she is gone. You hear the bedroom door shut. And you sit there staring at the television which is now clear with a Cher infomercial, muted. Then you hear noises, almost a thumping. It's Lula.

She comes from the opposite end of the trailer and is clutching a book close to her Garth Brooks T-shirt. She looks like she hasn't combed her hair in days and probably hasn't. Her glasses are hanging so close to the edge of her nose that they could fall off at any moment.

"What are you reading?"

"The new Carole Stein mystery. I can't wait to see what happens next." This is her favorite statement.

"What's happening to you?" you ask, trying to be polite. "Since last spring at the community college, you've just sat around reading."

"Is that a bad thing?"

"No, but you never leave. You used to have so many friends and you just, I don't know, lived."

She walks over and kisses you on the cheek and puts her hand on your thick brown hair. "I'm fine, Dad. I'm just thinking a lot lately about things that only I can. I gave you my financial aid refund check to pay for that new old jalopy of a truck you're driving. I'm not doing nothing. It might look that way, but I'm not."

"So there's nothing wrong with you?"

"No, not really, except for the same thing that's wrong with you," she says wisely, walking away. "And someday, it'll all work itself out." She heads toward the kitchen.

"There's some cobbler."

"No, thanks. Just need my Diet Coke," she says, using only the refrigerator light as a guide. "Do you want anything while I'm here?"

You shake your head, but realize she can't see you. "No."

"Are you fucked up again?" she asks, gazing into your eyes. As if she can tell if you're high or not.

You nod and she smiles. "Gotta get back to this book."

She moves heavily down the hallway carrying two liters of Diet Coke, leaving you alone with plants and a single goldfish.

Then you open the window.

2

You are in your denim jacket, pulling a way-too-small bottle out of the left pocket. You take another Valium and wash it down with Jägermeister. You have to be careful. This combination, it can kill.

You sit down on the yellow carpet that was once shaggy and watch the television, growing more fucked up. Beside the light from the television, the only other light is coming from the cheap lamp Gina bought in Mexico. You lie there, staring up, wondering why the roof of this place hasn't caved in. While the rest of the trailer is deteriorating, the ceiling has remained fine. You wait, wondering if this will be the night it crumbles. Even a small chunk of plaster would be a start.

Floors are good things, it's just getting up from them that you find to be the problem. And you realize you have forgotten about the aquarium. Maybe it even has more light than anything else in the house. This is what drives you to get up and turn off that covered-wagon lamp and the television. The light is right now, coming only from the aquarium.

You can't believe that you have lived here so long. You had dreamed of a mansion on the edge of New Orleans or Malibu, not a trailer in Mississippi. You take another sip of the Jägermeister and stretch a little. Restlessness, you have discovered, is not a virtue.

Spread out on the floor near the couch, you think about Gina in that room past the kitchen, waiting for her life to suddenly become good. Now that you barely speak to each other, staying married is just one of those things that you do. Gina was like that even in college. You knew that she would be. You were the leaver. You'd be the one to break her heart. But instead of doing it in one fell swoop, years ago, you have turned it into a life-

17

time departure. You wonder what it must be like for her, watching someone slowly burn away.

Now that all of the pills and drink have kicked in, you find yourself able to breathe. Things in the living room become strange in the light, larger than they actually are. Everything is doubling and tripling in size. But you're not so fucked up that you don't realize that it's all in your head. In fact, you're only halfway to where you want to be tonight.

More than anything else, the light from the fish tank illuminates the other side of the room, across from the couch. The shadows of the bubbles dance along the wall. Still you can see the encyclopedia, which goes from A to AC, and realize that it isn't balancing the couch as well as you thought it was. That's when you turn and look at the trees and realize that they are not just big, but that they've overtaken the room. And that's why you freeze.

You know the best thing to do is to go to sleep, but you're too wired, even considering everything that's in you. You have to stay awake, just in case. Just in case of whatever.

When you came back from the war, you said that you'd never end up like this. But during these moments, when you're high, you slip back in time. It seems like only ten minutes have passed since you were shot, since you were young. At this moment, it could be 1969 or 1970, or later and later, or earlier and earlier. These are the things that you think about when you are perfectly fucked up and perfectly alone.

In the kitchen you find a butcher knife in the drain board. You don't want to open and close any drawers or cabinet doors and awaken Gina or Lula.

In the living room, you begin to cut the large plant you hate so much. And then cut a little more and then you stop about halfway, leaving bits of strong green against a dying yellow. Definitely enough for Gina to notice in the morning. Everything is small again, or at least back to its normal size. Even the front door. You take your flannel shirt even though you want to feel the air at night. When you open the front door, you realize that your tolerance is increasing again. You feel no pain, but you're not as fucked up as you could be. Still, you hold back from taking anything else. Tonight, you are determined to stop before being stopped.

You walk down the steps and it is like doing some sort of weird dance that you feel completely in control of, knowing it is graceful in its own strange way. Knowing that if you keep doing it long enough, one of these nights it is going to lead to your resurrection.

3

You push the button on the front door of Jack's Place and wait to be buzzed in. This is how it works here in this place that looks like a small brick house with crepe paper and a disco ball. It's on the same highway where you had both of your wrecks. A curvy road which could send even a sober person into a deep ditch if they weren't aware of the turns. You stand staring for quite a while at the cheap year-round Christmas lights which line the window. Part of you wants to turn around and leave, but finally the bartender recognizes you from beyond the glass door and buzzes you in.

You immediately take a seat at the corner of the main bar as Max, the bald bartender, dances your way. Something from *Rocky Horror* is on, and though you've always hated it, right now such things you can overlook. You know it will get better. It's this hope that's gotten you into trouble in the past.

"Whiskey." That's all that you say to him. He is all pierced and you wonder what it must be like for him to walk through the aisles of the stores in town, or even to go to the bank with his shaved head and thrice-pierced right ear. He is older than you and owns the place. You wonder if he's making any money. Even though there are quite a few people here for a Sunday night, you know that most people are still scared to park their pick-up trucks outside and come in.

The place smells only a little like a bar, not like the ones in New Orleans. This is more like a brick house with jukebox and dime-store decorations. It's a retreat. But a place like this, in a town like this, is a little scary. It's like camping outdoors, in a place where bears can come ravage your tent at any moment. Buy the whiskey, and the feeling of not being alone makes you feel braver.

You look around and see that there are many people here your age, none of whom you recognize. It just feels good to be here. Breathing is still difficult, but easier than at home.

The windows of the place are all covered with fake velvet curtains. There are even bars on them, to keep certain dangerous animals out. Each time somebody is buzzed in, you like the way the breeze feels from outside.

"You can handle this?" Max asks.

"Oh, yeah..."

"You know what, Gary, I was thinking. I will definitely know when you and your wife break up."

"How?"

"You'll start drinking beer."

This isn't funny to you at first, then you get it, so you laugh. And you think that he is laughing, too, but when you look up, he is at the other end of the bar, tending to others. Your laughter turns to a proud smile as you take a drink.

After a while, you feel ridiculous and lonely sitting at the bar. So you get up and begin to move around the place. It's big and tacky and open and poorly lit, like a Bingo Palace. In fact, you are sure that your mother dragged you and Gina here to play Bingo in the late seventies. None of you won.

There are booths against the back wall. That's where you want to be. While everyone is checking specific people out, you sit in your corner booth and watch them all do what they do to get what they want. It's embarrassing for you that at forty-five, you don't entirely understand the whole scene. Not feeling comfortable in a gay bar is almost like going to a high-school prom alone.

There is a pool table nearby, electronic lottery machines; and despite that huge disco ball, nobody's dancing. You can't understand why there's no one under the ball, flickering beneath its rotation.

The booth you have taken has an air conditioner next to it. Just one of those little window units. And you know it's chilly outside, but you're getting hot, so you reach over and turn it on low. There are paper streamers that blow from the sides of the vent. You sink into that ripped, red booth. In this place, especially in this booth, it is okay to be alone. Home.

Somebody plays something from a musical, and you hate musicals, so you have no choice but to get up and move to the jukebox. There are actually some people dancing now, but too near the booth that you feel is your own. You're afraid that they'll sit. If they do, you'll have no choice but to take a seat on the floor beside one of the electronic slot machines. Home, indeed.

You motion to Max, dancing behind the bar in his way-too-tight black leather. He looks out for you because you talked your boss into giving him a discount on his carpentry work. He usually drives around Petulia in his convertible. Not to show off; just as a reminder to the town, and probably to himself, that he exists. "Remembering you have a voice in the South is important," he once said to you, one of the few full quotations you have ever remembered. As you flip through the jukebox, you hope that one of those cute brave hearts out there dancing hasn't played the whole soundtrack to this musical.

You go the bar and there is a group of younger people there, all dressed the same. Khakis and button-down shirts. They're drinking wine. They are all good-looking, and while they don't look exactly the same, it's still like they are each the same person. Their hair is so short. They seem so dressed up to be out in a place like this on a Sunday night. You wonder why they aren't in the French Quarter. These days, people must always feel the need to dress up. Each party is always potentially the last.

As you drink the enormous shot Max pours, you

wonder if you'll ever lose your hair, if you'll ever look like him, if you'll ever be him.

"You are beautiful!" Beauty? A hand is on your arm. It's one of the khakied boys and since they are all so alike, you can't tell which one has said it. Finally you realize it's the one with the longish hair.

You pull away and nod and say "thank you" so softly that you are sure none of them hear you. You want to fuck one of them, just not enough to go through with it at the moment. It is sort of like with Gina, except this time you really want it.

You go to the bathroom for a Valium snack. On your way there, you hear someone begging for some Madonna to be played. You smile because you know that your selection will beat theirs to the air. You played Traffic. This is the wonderful thing about jukeboxes, finding a song that doesn't belong in a particular setting.

In that small bathroom, there are things written all over the wall like "Call me, I'm fully broken in..." and dozens of phone numbers.

And there is a mirror. You grab both sides of the dingy sink and look into the mirror. Beauty? You wonder if it is possible for someone to think that you are as good-looking as Gina did at LSU. Though your hair is still thick and your body feels thin, you're not sure if what you see is what exists. You know that the grayness will spread from your fingers and overtake your last youthful image. Since you know that's what's coming, you see an old man in the mirror, sure that's what everyone else sees, too. At this moment, your eyes grow smaller, then big again, animated, as though someone is drawing them, then changing their minds about how they should be.

And you can't stop going deeper into your own eyes. You see yourself, but don't feel your body. You have stunned yourself with the way your image can change forms. Many people you've been appear in that mirror.

First, you as a blood-stained soldier with the grimy wall behind you becoming a forest. Then, as a lost man in the French Quarter with your dick hanging out, a confused look enveloping your face. At one point, your image in the mirror has closed eyes, but you can still see yourself, passed out in a ditch somewhere along a deserted highway.

People come in and out of the bathroom. They look at you strangely, bump into you, try to strike up conversations, or yell at your for blocking the sink. But you are so taken with the dark images of yourself that you don't completely hear or understand them. And you've lost all track of time, which is passing quickly. You don't realize how urgently the night is moving, propelling you forward without your even knowing it. Though two hours pass, blacking out has never been so fast or colorful.

As you stand, gripping the sink, the door suddenly opens and makes a loud noise, shaking you from this state of awakened sleep. It happens so fast that you jump, coming to and recognizing who has entered. A safe animal has come into the tent. You are afraid at first. Then your eyes meet in the mirror and finally Will, a sheriff's deputy, speaks. "I've always told you, Gary, that if I looked like you," he says, "I wouldn't worry about a thing."

You turn around to this man who is holding out a hand. He is pretty handsome, maybe even more so than in high school, where he'd dropped out early after getting the cheerleading captain pregnant. "I won't tell if you don't," he says, still holding out his hand.

When you shake his hand, you expect it to be stronger. On the right hand, the one you shake, there is this thing. Not just a sore, it goes beyond that. You know what it is. Purple lesions, purple hearts.

"Your secret is safe with me," you say. Then you both pull away awkwardly and suddenly have the urge to hide your own hands. But you stop when you realize that he's watching you do this. "I feel like we're suppose to ask each other about our wives," you joke, hoping it's funny.

He shrugs. "What's the point?"

You join him at the urinal to pee, neither one of you even looking below the other's bellybutton. "I'm glad I ran into somebody I know. It's very lonely out there."

"Shucks, man," he begins, "I was at the bar for the longest time. I gotta get goin' though. Got work to do."

"Are you on duty now?"

"Naw, in about an hour I go on."

And your eyes hit again and you know he is a different kind of animal, not one that rips tents down. "I guess not," you say.

You shake hands again, both of you too fucked up to worry about washing them.

"See ya."

Before you can catch the door, it shuts, leaving you alone with a poster of a shirtless man in tight black pants. If he would step out of the poster, something sexual could happen. You're not sure exactly of what, but something could occur.

You know that you are holding up well tonight because when you get back to the bar, Max pours you another drink. "Don't fall too far off the wagon," he teases.

The place is clearing out. No one is dancing and you see that the booth is still yours. All of your songs have ended. You missed them by losing yourself in the bathroom. Donna Summer is on. You hated disco in 1979, but somehow now it sounds all right. Almost good.

Sitting there, you watch the Budweiser clock tick away. This you find is so much better than watching infomercials all night long. So much better than sleep. Then a song comes on the jukebox that you were too sick of to play yourself. But you're glad someone else did. "Just yesterday mornin'," you hum along hoping nobody can hear you. This song takes you back, past Jackson Browne, past LSU, Gina, and American life in the summertime. Vietnam, 1969.

You are freezing by the air conditioner. The place is virtually empty now. Even the preppie kids are going away. They are so good to look at, and one of them has even played Janis Joplin. And the one that did, wants to stay. He is yelling at his friends. "I want to hear the rest of my fucking songs!" But you can see how he thinks that he is going to be left, so he goes with them. They leave like triplets, with Janis Joplin's "Cry Baby" following them into the Southern night.

Someone over there in Vietnam had first turned you onto Janis Joplin's music. And you used to disco dance to it before there was such a thing.

The only people in the bar at this point are the real alcoholics, five altogether. You are hunched over the table in your familiar way. Gina once said that when you sit like this you look like you are protecting yourself and letting your guard down at the same time. Always waiting for the attack. Even in the army, standing up straight was something you always fought.

In the darkness of the bar with your John Deere cap pulled low, you wonder if the other people in the place can hear your thoughts. Maybe they can't see through the cap, maybe sliding further down in the booth helps. You're glad that you've worn your flannel shirt. It is thick, hopefully nobody can penetrate it.

The disco ball is still spinning as you take your last two pills for the night. When you first came in, the ball was silver, now it is every color. The place is smelling more like a Bingo Hall now, with a ton of whiskey thrown in for all of the ladies who years ago sat around waiting for G-56. You wash the pills down with whiskey.

You'd first discovered whiskey, like Janis Joplin, in the army with your buddy Kevin. He was from New York of all places, and sometimes after you'd sucked each other off, you'd find ways to press your boots together in a way that only the two of you understood. Since he was from the city, you felt like a real hick around him sometimes. It was like he was so much stronger. That's why you were surprised when he got hit.

People were yelling and dropping and firing, and you just stopped and knelt down beside him, not worrying about being hit. You know a person is dead when everything inside is sticking out and all over the ground. Like when your father first took you to skin a deer. You just watched as his beauty left him and turned to that fiery end-of-life stench that had become the incense of a day in the jungle. From his chest, you saw his ribs and you reached down and touched one. Bones. You wanted to touch his ribs some more.

Years later, when you told Gina, she thought that it was disgusting. But it was all that you had left of him. When blood gets on you, it stays, even after you wash it off. His feet were the only thing unscathed. Toe-tags.

You are still sitting there, hovering over your empty glass. Looking around, you see everything in the room become three. You are almost there. It is the only way to push yesterday further back. Gunned down.

In the corner booth, you are choking on all of this. Especially the memories and drugs and drink and the way the place keeps changing shapes. You want to stand, but either you grow smaller or the booth grows bigger. So you stay there.

The floor becomes closer. Darkness, as you know all too well, rises. The tile is cold. Home?

"Just yesterday mornin'," you think you say again and again.

4

"Good morning," this lanky boy says to you from across a faded room. It's one of those rooms where the sunlight is the only thing that keeps things visibly yellow. The boy is tall and skinny, and you're not sure if you've ever seen him before in your life. He's dressed, and you could swear that the clothes that he is wearing are yours, but they are not. Something silver hangs from the end of his neck. Dog tags.

You cannot stop looking at him. You are in this tiny apartment filled with milk-crate bookshelves and posters of paintings. One of them is gray, with a single, even grayer bird falling from the sky. There is a mattress on the floor, and this is where you are lying. It is almost comfortable, but you know that you have to get up. Still you stare at him, your eyes opening and closing, photographing him as you are too tired to move. He looks young, too young for you to be in this bed with, while you should be at work. His blond hair is uncombed, his eyes so wonderfully small that you wonder how they can see a thing. And he moves quickly around the room, stopping briefly to look at you as though you have always been there.

"Where am I?" you finally ask.

"You were so fucked up last night," he says. "I didn't know what was happening, but I knew that someone had to help you. So that's what I did. I helped you."

"What time is it?"

"Noon."

"Oh, man!" Your head hurts when you sit up, but your mind is racing because you're late for work, and Gina will be there to deal with when you get home.

"Everything's cool. I just brought you here and you

slept. Well, you had confused dreams, but mostly you slept."

"And where did you sleep?"

"I didn't. I stayed awake writing to old friends. Since there's nothing else to do around here, I write. I only sleep to dream."

"What do you write about?"

"Everything."

"What do you dream about?"

"Nose rings, Impressionist winters, 1979."

"How old are you?

"Old. What's your name?"

"Gary."

"I'm Zachary." He holds out his hand and you shake it. His fingers are long, like he could reach two octaves on a piano.

"Did we do anything last night?"

"I told you. I wrote. And you lost your mind a little."

"Again," you groan.

"It's okay," he says, seeming to grow taller and skinnier. "I do it, too."

"Do what?"

"Go crazy. I've made a life of it." He sits down behind his scratched-up desk. "Use whatever you need. There's aspirin in the bathroom, Coke in the fridge..." In a flannel shirt, his blond hair almost the color of the paneling, you feel his eyes studying you.

"I don't need anything," you say, rising, looking at the gray poster on the wall, knowing you shouldn't be distracted by such things when you are already so late for a day in your life.

"You like it?" he sounds excited.

"Yeah."

"It's this thing I got at this opening in New York. Ross Bleckner is the artist. You should see his other stuff in color. It's like you can't tell whether or not the birds are rising or falling. You're the first person around here to even notice it."

Then he stands up and walks closer. You're managing to get your shoes on now. When you stand in your white T-shirt, and khakis, you initially seem just a little shorter than he is, then you both seem the same size.

"You've been to New York?" you ask.

"I used to live there. It's no big deal, not the way people make it sound. It's just another place. Different, but still just a place."

He takes a step closer to you. His lips. They are full and red against his pale skin. You know that you probably look like shit.

"I hate to be rude," he says, "but I wait tables at Johnny's, and I have to be there soon. But you can stay and get cleaned up before you leave. The door locks automatically."

He blinks slowly and touches your shirt, like he's never touched blue flannel before. "Nice meeting you," he says slowly, his Southern drawl finally showing as he walks toward the door. Beautiful, you think. And you wonder where he comes from and exactly where he's been...

It was a brutal winter when Zachary left New York and Girgio, the professor, behind. It snowed until April. Snowfall records broke and the cracks in their relationship become wider. But it wasn't supposed to be that way. Because these months also contained scenes that Zachary had dreamed of when he was younger. There were dinner parties where everyone drank too much red wine, with Zachary always drinking just a couple of glasses more than everyone else. He would sit there raking his fingernails across the tablecloth as though it were blank, as though there were nothing to be knocked over. Sometimes he'd have his friends join these dinner parties, mostly girls. They would just all get drunk and stare at each other, all afraid to speak, for fear of being cut down. So they just looked at each other, and he'd feel like an idiot for trying to mix artists and physicists.

After dinner, there were cigars smoked as he sat in a room full of intellectuals with whom he couldn't keep up. He'd sit there as they tore everyone to bits. And he'd watch them as their glasses of Calvados grew empty and he'd keep serving them. Pouring for them, then for himself again. It was the only thing he knew how to do correctly during these times. Brilliant people from far away countries would ask him questions, not knowing that if Zachary answered wrongly, Girgio would immediately pounce on him, hitting him below the belt. Even the most mundane questions, the ones which Zachary was sure he knew the answer to, would tremble out like he was completely stupid.

And sometimes, when he'd had enough, when he was sure he was right about something, he'd just let go. It was definitely the alcohol that let him cut loose. But the alcohol also made him wonder the following day if he knew what he was saying made any sense at all. And if he said too much, if he got carried way, Girgio would go crazy after all the guests had left. His dark Italian eyes would grow bigger and Zachary would find himself on the defense. Sometimes the professor would push him and he'd step back, finding himself sliding down one of the white walls.

He didn't know what else to do, so he'd sit there in that big West Village apartment, with a glass in his hand, wondering why the lamps were growing so drowsy, wondering why the red sun had gone down, like the wine had so easily earlier that day. He was sure that the snow would never stop. New York winter had become something of an icy otherworld. There were times when he actually believed that New York City would stay white forever. That much snow could never just disappear. Seasons changing had replaced his earlier fantasies of the glamorous life in New York.

On some occasions, like the one where a whole group of various "them"s from the university and a few friends were meeting for dinner at a Russian restaurant uptown, he'd call Amy from work. And because she knew the streets better than he did, she would lead him in her short, blonde, waifish way to the East Village to go beyond Calvados and shell steak. And someone standing by a garbage can would say "blue" and they would say "boy," then an exchange was made. He'd then walk her to the F train to Brooklyn with their bags of dope, which had the "Blue Boy" logo on them.

"You're so lucky," she said, "all these fancy restaurants and foreign people."

"I'll see you tomorrow at work," he said, watching her glide, hidden in her big black coat, down the steps to a world of trains that he still hadn't figured out the routes of.

He still had a dorm room at the time, but he only went there to do lines and listen to really loud music. This night, the night of the Russian restaurant, he went to that dorm room on Eighth Street. And after he put on some vintage Psychedelic Furs, he stuck the straw into the bag, unaware of exactly how much he was doing. And he sat back against the hard scratchy mattress, but didn't fall backward. Things were spinning, but it didn't feel so bad, things were just a little out of line before diving nose-first into the waxed-paper bag. For the first time, since he'd started doing drugs, especially heroin, he thought maybe he'd overdone it. His heart was not beating fast or slow, but like the room, something just wasn't right with it.

"Love My Way" was on. He sat there until the song was over. While he still felt a little nauseated, he had settled down into what could be considered a comfortable high. He looked at the alarm clock, knowing he would be late as usual. He still had to take time out to throw up before dinner.

And dinner went fine with that group of people that night. They were the types of people who sent the wine back, but never said "thank you" to the waiter. One of the women at the table asked him once if he was feeling all right. He lied and said "yes" and sat there as they all talked about tenure and food and Paris in the summer. It was snowing again, and he was so glad that he had a view of the window. Because the snow was actually interesting right now. It drowned the others out, and he had his own silent conversations with it. Zachary was simply cordial that night and never exploded.

Back home, he wondered if Girgio was onto him. If he knew that he was high. Instead, he seemed to be on cloud nine himself, pulling Zachary close. "Was I okay tonight?" he asked. "I felt kind of nauseated. That's why I didn't say much."

"You were perfect."

"But I hardly said a word."

"That's why you were perfect."

He felt the professor's familiar hands holding onto him, not letting him go, slipping down below the back of his khakis.

"Yes," Zachary said, out of boredom, out of habit. "Fuck me."

And as he lay there across the rough couch getting fucked from behind, he looked around the white apartment, all high, his eyes still half-opened, waiting for it to be over. Knowing all along how, one of these days, his heart was either going to simply give out or change directions. When Girgio came, groaning a little, Zachary was thinking, "Someday I'm just not going to be here anymore."

5

Building houses is what you do and during the day hammers and nails almost take the place of pills and booze. It's been a few hours since you've left that young man's house, and you are on your lunch break, sitting on the top of the roof of this house you're building in a subdivision just outside of Petulia. It's one of those neighborhoods where everyone has so much money that you can't figure out why they want to live so close to each other. A lot of them move here to escape New Orleans, but you don't see the difference between living in a crowded city of possibilities to a crowded sub-division where every move you make seems to be preset in stone. In towns like this, people read you like a book that they've only thought of opening. To these people, Petulia is the world.

You're eating a sandwich you picked up at the Piggly Wiggly. It's ham and cheese. Not bad. So much better than those that Gina buys at the new Wal-Mart Supercenter. You hate that place because it contains everything, and everybody goes there. On Sundays, Gina tries to drag you there, but usually you refuse. It's the sort of store where you can be sure to run into somebody you know but never thought you would see again. People from high school now work behind the counter, scan your items, and try to make small talk. Old teachers, old preachers that you lied to and said you had handed your life over to Jesus are always in and out of there. Wal-Mart is some sort of American dream that eludes you, so you stay out of there.

"Ten minutes," your boss says, from down below. His name is Richard. He's really red, beard and all. But it's nice that you can show up so late and still feel secure about having a job. And he blasts classic rock all day

34

long. It's become a little boring, those same old songs each day. You were longing for something new, but since you don't know where to look, you don't suggest that he change the station.

Like your father, you know that you're a good carpenter. Building houses for other people, for people who will move from the city to shop at Wal-Mart, fascinates you and makes you wonder why you can't be satisfied with what's been given to you. By building their houses, you're fitting into the mainstream as much as a person like you can.

This is one of the hotter days in October. You've taken off your flannel shirt and feel just right. You smell your armpits to see if the sweat has overtaken you. But you still smell good. You took a shower before you left that guy Zachary's house. It felt good to be in a new place, a new shower. It was a green shower and the curtain was one of those with a million colorful smiling faces. You could have stayed in there forever. There was nobody but you to stop the rain. Taking showers in somebody else's place always makes you fantasize that you are in a hotel in a place far away, a place where people like you make sense to those around you. But you feel a little guilty for having used up so much of Zachary's soap, leaving him only a think crescent of whiteness in the soap dish. Moonstruck.

"Crystal Blue Persuasion" comes on, and you are shocked that they are finally playing a song you like. You know that your break is over, so you move to the roof of long open spaces. Beams and ladders are your guides to the ground. Your tool belt feels heavier than usual. And suddenly, you feel your foot miss a beat, and you are out of sync with Tommy James and you find yourself flipping down, through the roof. Crashing your body could be even more exciting than crashing a truck.

But somewhere between the roof and the cement slab below, you stop and you swear it feels like several long minutes as you hover numbly, unable to feel your left hand, then your right. And you see Richard and your other two co-workers as they say "Gary," in a way that keeps you hanging there, with nothing to hold onto. If there were people inside of those straw huts you burned down so many years ago, it must have been like this as they suddenly lost all feeling, then died.

The ground is only about ten feet below, but still it seems like miles. You wonder if you'll ever hit the ground. You wonder what it will feel like. But this in-between feels fresh, and it seems to go on for a great deal of time.

Before they get the ladder to you, the song on the radio ends, the feeling returns to every part of your body, and you begin to fall more swiftly to the ground below. You wonder which way you will land. Facedown could be the best way to go, so that's what you aim for, knowing that you'll never have to see the world again.

Your feet hit the ground. And there is a brief snap, and you are sure that you must be hurt, but after a few seconds realize that no part of you has been damaged. They are all standing around looking at you as if you've been killed. You don't even try to explain it to them, because to you it doesn't seem all that strange. Your body knows what it's doing in times like this.

You stand there, your feet firmly on the ground. "Are you all right, man?" asks Richard.

You nod, surprised that you are.

"I've never seen anything like that in my life," Jeff, an armed-robber-turned-carpenter says. "I can't believe that you aren't hurt."

You want to tell them that it happens all the time, just to really throw them off-guard and shut them up. But nothing exactly like this has ever occurred to you before, so you remain still for a few moments. "We should get back to work," you insist to Richard, as though you are his boss. Reluctantly, everybody does.

As you nail the afternoon away, you hit your thumb twice but don't quite feel it the way you usually do. The music keeps you humming along. While you work until sundown, building this house for future Wal-Mart customers, you think about how good a shower would be in that green bathroom of Zachary's. You think about how all hell is going to break loose at home and how Gina is probably already pulling down the roof, waiting until you get home so she can crucify you. Home-wrecking.

But mostly you spend the day waiting for the sun to end, full of regret. Not because you didn't die facedown on the concrete, or because you've no doubt disappointed Gina again.

Instead you regret that, earlier in the day, you wanted to touch Zachary's shirt the way he touched yours, but were afraid to. Like pressing boots against boots, you were afraid the whole world would have seen. Shielding rears its animalistic face. The face is yours. Guarded.

6

There is a lot of commotion when you get home. Boxes are piled in front of the trailer, and you know that Gina's obviously had enough. You've finally pushed her too far, and you feel sick for it. The truck is noisy and you know that they can hear you when you pull up. You still smell like Zachary's disappearing soap.

Opening the front door is walking straight into uncertainty. "What's going on?" you ask.

Gina is at the kitchen table reading a *True Romance* magazine. There are boxes all around, full of things, but the furniture in intact. You know you have to speak first. It's the least you can do. "What's going on?"

"I tried talking to her, but you know how she is." Gina looks refreshed, not like she's been up all night waiting for you.

"Who?"

"Lula. She's got some crazy idea that she's just gonna jump in a car with one of those queers from New Orleans and move to the French Quarter." She puts down her magazine and looks at you. "She can't just run off like that."

"Why not?"

Gina shoves her chair back and stands up, throwing her hands in the air, looking exactly like her mother, a woman crossing a line that only she can understand. "You're as crazy as her. You don't just pick up and leave like that. How will she survive?"

"Where is she?"

"In her room. Maybe you can talk some sense into her."

You doubt that you can, and almost don't feel that you need to. "Lula," you say tapping on the door lightly.

"Come on in," she says energetically, like she's not

doing anything out of the ordinary.

Her room smells like a library and melting scented candles. But mostly it's bare now. She actually looks better, like she has bathed and put on some decent clothes. "So you're leaving."

"You won't believe what happened. You remember my friend Justin, right?"

"The one who has a shrine to Madonna in his bedroom?"

"No, that's Carl." She's still packing things in a very disorganized way. "Justin's the one that manages a bar in the French Quarter. Well, guess what?" She actually claps her hands. Happiness. "He's got me a job there. And he says that I can stay with him until I get a place of my own."

Her room is so empty now. You can remember how only days ago it was lined with books and posters of bands you had never heard of. Her dresser seems strange, being all empty. Before, she had so many crosses hanging along the mirror above it that it was impossible to see your reflection. But now the space is vacant. The only thing above the dresser is a hole in the wall, where maybe she punched the wall out of anger years ago. This trailer is slowly falling apart. Straw huts.

"Here," you say, taking out your wallet and pulling out the credit card that has the most available credit. "In case you need anything. Use it."

She reaches over and hugs you as you sit on the bare mattress. "At least you're not being like her." She is referring to Gina, who is yelling at herself in the kitchen.

"It sounds like fun. I wish it was me. Just go and come back if you have to. At least now you're doing something."

"Thanks, Dad."

"So, what bar is this?"

"It's called Barracuda. It's a really busy place. Lots of money to be made while I figure out what I really want to do."

She stands up, and grabs the copy of *The Rose*, throwing it roughly into a cardboard box. "What kind of soap did you use? You smell great."

"Just soap," you say, surprised that the green shower experience is still with you. "Call us when you get there. We'll worry, you know."

There is silence as she takes one of the wooden crosses with Jesus hanging from it and puts it around your neck. "I love you, Daddy."

"You are the one that is loved," you say. "Even by her." You motion toward the door, though Gina's yelling has stopped.

"I know," Lula says, beginning to move quicker than you've ever seen her move. When she moves with speed, she seems slimmer. "Justin will be here any minute. I don't want him to have to wait."

"Then finish packing and get the fuck out of here. Serve a Hurricane for me," you say as you leave the room. "At least once a day when you serve one of them, think about your Petuliaed-out dad."

"I will," she says, knowing that she'll go through with it.

You leave, aware that nobody will ever be able to fill that room the way she has. While you know that nobody will ever be able to fill this room like her, you also realize that it's the best thing that's ever happened for Lula. Escape.

In the living room, you find Gina just sitting there in the recliner. You're surprised that she hasn't mentioned your not coming home last night. You walk over and sit on the arm of the chair, waiting for her to ask where you were last night. Instead, she begins to touch your hands, then your face. You know that mentioning your slight headache will complicate things. The cross that Lula gave you hangs heavily around your neck.

"You feel like you have a fever." Her right hand is

placed firmly against your forehead. "You're burning up."

She gets up and goes to the kitchen as you kick back in the chair. You'll want a pill soon, any pill. You hear her in the kitchen and you know she's getting the thermometer. She returns with the digital one and places it under your tongue.

Like a child, you sit as a series of beeps ends with a long drawn out one. Feeling hot is something you're used to, and assume that she is, too.

"No. It's normal. You don't have a fever. Nothing's wrong with you at all. How can you not have a fever and yet feel so feverish when I touch you?"

"I don't know."

She is standing over you like she's expecting you to tell her where you were without her asking. "The fever I have," you finally say, "can't be measured by that thing." She takes a few steps back like she foolishly believes that you can set her on fire or something.

"What?"

"It can't be measured by anything. I just keep getting more and more warm." Human combustion.

"Maybe you need to go talk to that man at the hospital again. In fact, Lula needs to go talk to somebody, too. You're both out of your minds. I yell and yell and still you just keep acting the same way. Both of you."

"Maybe I need to explode," you say.

She shakes her head and walks back into the kitchen, where she stays until a car horn calls Lula from outside. Lula runs noisily to the front door. "He's here!" she exclaims, running outside.

Gina looks at you, afraid to come closer, afraid of you giving her the disease that begins with a fire in the brain before spreading.

In that recliner, you rock slowly, holding onto the cross, wondering what it would be like to hang in midair and explode in the same day. It scares you to think about it. You sit quietly and try and cool off a bit, afraid of what will happen if you have another night like the previous one. Flammability tempts.

7

Lula was born twenty years ago. She'd been conceived during one of your early seventies breakdowns, when they were still a new thing for you. Your suspicions of Gina's affairs were sometimes a bigger issue than your ability to lose your touch with reality. Though it would have been physically impossible for anyone of Lula's size to come from such thin people, nobody in your families ever said a word about it. Though Lula must have known that she wasn't yours, she never asked questions about it. She didn't know that her real father was Cecile Middleton, the hugely spirited, hugely sized, married, high school principal. Accused of sexually harassing a teacher, he lost his job shortly after Gina became pregnant, forcing him and his wife to move away to Texas.

Though Lula never discussed it, sometimes when you would look at her as she drank her Diet Coke, after you'd had too many pills, she'd say that she understood you. And you took that to mean that she literally meant everything, even the fact that she couldn't possibly be your biological daughter. It was one of those things that was unspoken when all three of you were in the house and not a noise was being made. What had started out as a secret had become an understanding. Silence speaks.

Now she is gone. It is 2 a.m., and you are still rocking in the chair, listening to a station that plays only music from the seventies. For some reason you don't feel like moving. Immobilized. You aren't even in the mood to go out, not even to buy a bottle of liquor, so you take two of your dwindling white pills. Bread is on singing "Everything I Own." Music that was once bad sounds good now, but makes you feel flattened by listening to it.

Gina is already in bed, having gone there pissed off

as usual because Lula has left for New Orleans, for a bigger life. You know that Gina isn't angry because she will miss Lula all that much—maybe a little from the habit of having her around. But not the way that mothers are supposed to miss daughters.

After the song is over, you turn off the stereo and then you hear it. At first it scares you, because you think it's coming from Lula's room. It's a noise, sounding not unlike funeral music to you, yet so much less harsh. You walk guardedly through the darkened hallway, where Lula used to dwell. She's left the light on. And there's nothing left there anymore, except the cheap furniture and empty Diet Coke bottles. Before you turn the light off, you notice that she's left the window open. It's better than a goodbye note to a would-be father, better than leaving that copy of *The Rose* behind. Air.

After you've turned off the light, you are sure the music will stop. It sounds like it's coming from far away, but not so far that you can't touch some of it. You walk to the window and suddenly there is silence. Maybe Gina was right, maybe it's time to go back to the hospital. Before when you heard things you were either fucked up or they were by Jefferson Airplane. You haven't heard music so foreign since Vietnam. You haven't heard something so undetectably frightening since certain swamps, where you wanted the snakes to get you before the Viet Cong.

Out of protection, you close the window and decide that bed might be the best answer. There is nothing better to do. Overdoing last night has tamed you for at least twenty-four hours. You're still surprised, almost frightened, that Gina hasn't mentioned it. You figure it's because she was too busy going on about Lula. But usually Gina, when she gets mad, can take on all subjects at once. Fighting every fight. Starting new wars.

You knock over a kitchen chair and leave it there. Tomorrow you'll pick it up before work. It will be a reason to rise. You have a glass of water at the sink and down two blues and hear it again. The music is back, and this time you realize it's not coming from the direction of Lula's room at all, but driving straight through the center of the trailer where you stand. You must ignore these things; the doctors have told you to. They all think you're crazier than you are. You know when you're flipping out. You've done it enough times. This time, you're just not going to think about hearing things, or what they mean. Instead you focus on how easy it is to swallow pills and hear music, no matter where it comes from.

Going to sleep seems like such a waste of time when all it leads to is picking up that chair tomorrow and building houses as the holes in your home increase. Still you head for the bedroom, where you expect the usual Gina, all beautiful in her nightgown, needing nothing more than to be held. That is what you always offer her. Not enough.

But the bed is empty. The window is open with its light-blue curtains, so transparent that most people would never have such ones in their bedroom. As they blow, you stand amazed; not since the early seventies, before Lula was born, have you found a bed still so firmly made. Outside the music seems louder, then you realize that it never actually stopped; it just decreased then increased in volume. At the window you stand, looking out into the cool night, seeing Gina's Volkswagen Rabbit gone.

You feel abandoned, though you have no right to. Betrayal has bred itself in you through silence. You've never felt this alone, not even in a corner booth or a ripped recliner. All of your silence is coming back at you from a distance, in a music that you can't comprehend. In a language that you don't speak.

The swamp water was thick over there in that other land, but you always knew that you'd find death in it, whether it was you or somebody else. Walking into this bedroom, you never imagined the waters could grow so murky or that voices from a foreign land would call out to you from an open field. This is a killing.

You hold onto both sides of the window. At least there is no jungle to block your view of the open highway, the open field across the way, where a woman's voice is so pure, you are actually beginning to feel a little for her. You still don't understand what she is saying, but you know that if you hold tightly enough, long enough to the storm windows, that you will be drawn in. It's the sort of music that your music teacher in grade school, the one who complimented the length of your fingers, listened to. This momentary death Gina has revenged you with, will somehow pass. You wonder if Gina has sneaked out as many nights as you.

A pickup truck passes by and it looks like yours, only newer and less noisy. As soon as it has passed, the music reaches one of those points again where you are sure that it has ended. Then it picks up, vibrantly.

You put your left foot out the window, then the right. The grass is cold, the dew wetting your mismatched socks. You ruin all of your good khakis by stupid adventures like this. But being called is different from simply being sung to.

In Vietnam, the prostitutes looked beautiful to you and you wanted to make love to them, and when you couldn't, you'd still pay them. The beauty wasn't just in them physically, it was in the way that you knew they would hold onto your whiteness, the way that you have held onto Gina all these years. You heard that there were male prostitutes, but the only time you saw one the language seemed too different. At the time, all Asian men looked like your death. But the women in the streets would speak a seductive language that made you want to walk into them and give them what they needed. Not necessarily economically or sexually, just in some way that only you could. But the language scared you. You never really knew if they were saying what you thought they were. You couldn't tell the difference between the words of prostitutes and those that were yelled when you and your platoon set a village on fire, afterwards hearing grandfathers and mothers and children crying out from straw huts, singing the same words: "Save me."

Outside you begin to cross the highway, walking deeper into the music, wondering whom Gina is seeing, more out of curiosity than jealousy. You hear the music calling more now, only now you know it wants you and you want it.

At some point, a cop car comes speeding down the road. They own the roads in towns like this. You are nearly across the ditch by the low wire fence when the cop car slows down and you know you're in trouble. So you stop, trapped. You almost immediately raise your hands, but instead stay frozen like a snowman from where there was actually rare snow in Mississippi. The cop car stays still.

The music is at a point now where you know that if you don't reach it, you never will. It is coming from that field and without Gina to habitually hold onto, or Lula to understand the insomnia, you have to get to the music.

Then because something has to be done, you do it. It is obvious that the car won't move, so for some reason you raise your hands slightly, but not all the way up, only halfway, above your sides. Just when you think that you've given in to the man with the powerful car, something unusual occurs. You see the cop, whoever it is, from the front seat raise his hands in the same way and after a few seconds drive off.

You step across the fence and walk toward the music, but it seems to be moving away. You actually begin to run after it. When you are nearly in the center of the field, you stumble to the ground. You think that you see a figure in the distance at the other end of the field, but because the moon is only a crescent, it is too dark to tell. In fact, the more you look, the more it looks like more than one person, but it could be the faraway pine trees, walking away with the music that has drawn you here.

You lie spread out there on the ground, grain-staining your clothes, knowing that this must seem crazy to anyone who would happen to witness it. But right now it makes so much sense to you that you almost want to laugh. The music is gone and you remember how bad you are at learning other languages. It's the reason you never finished LSU. It's the reason you can't talk to Gina, or even Lula, unless you're completely fucked up. It's the reason you couldn't save those people who begged you in that country far away, the reason you can't put out the fire from the men and women who have been calling out your name for years. And the reason that after twenty-two years, you are able to rest outside alone. Using only yourself and memories of the music for your protection, you are able to sleep. Soundly.

8

Afterwards, you sleep for five straight nights with Gina as though nothing has happened. You've noticed how not mentioning things is like repeating them loudly. It's Friday night and you're not even having your pill-driven, drunken-type fun. You wonder if you go back to the bar, if Zachary will be there. But the possibility of new types of fun always scares you, makes your limbs stiffen. Change hurts.

Still, you feel that you are supposed to be doing something. Anything. It's one of those things that you thought you'd outgrow, but still you feel like you're supposed to be bringing flowers to skinny boys and spending the night drinking, watching a black-and-white movie with subtitles or going in some completely crazy direction. Over the edge.

You see Gina scraping dinner from the plates. It was a pot roast and good enough to help you hold an entire bottle of your choice. It's strange to watch her now. In her apron, her hair tied back, she still looks innocent at fifty. But you know that she sneaked out the other night. You wonder how many times she's done it before when you were out getting plastered. Dishonesty has never been a trait of hers, but you realize that you are not the one to judge on this particular subject. Tonight, you wonder which one of you will do it first. Escape having become like a board game in this house of silent knowledge. With Lula gone, it's like the whole board has unfolded. You and Gina are the only two players. You have no strategy, and you're sure that she doesn't either, but victory is in the mind. You don't care which one of you conquers, you just hope that somebody wins soon. Change exhausts.

"Have you ever seen that movie about the Kennedy

assassination?"

"No." You stand up, drinking a Coors, a light start for you.

"Well, I was thinking that maybe we could rent it."

You move around the kitchen, helping her load the dishwasher.

"Well, I was thinking that we could rent that or something tonight. It's so quiet around here."

You think about every door and window in the house. "It's a long movie, Gina."

"Oh, never mind."

"Maybe we could rent something else. What about *La Dolce Vita*?"

"What?"

"The Fellini movie about the reporter."

"Subtitles?"

"Yes."

She doesn't even have to say "no" to your movie choice, you know that you'll go back and forth like this until nothing is rented. It is times like this when you wonder how it's lasted all of these years. Silence.

The dishwasher is loaded and the washing detergent seems all clotted, but you manage to shake some of it out. Then you wonder what the difference is between this stuff and that which clothes are washed with.

"We could drive over to Mama's," she says. "She's been asking about you. We could do that."

"We could," you say, not meaning that you have any intentions of going there.

"Then let's go!" Her apron is off in what must be about two seconds and you can't believe that you've agreed to this, without really even agreeing to it. The story of your life. "I'll go get ready, then, okay?" She kisses you softly on the lips.

Of course that's when you start digging through the back of a corner cabinet. You surprisingly find a bottle with about ten blue Valium, and you take four. Your beer is getting hot, but it doesn't matter because it would take three six-packs to match the four pills you've swallowed.

You stand there looking out the kitchen window, wishing that you could mention the field music to Gina, wishing that she could not simply get it, but really get it. You look out to where, there in the darkness, you slept those few nights ago. Waking with the sun that day had been the most nonannoying alarm clock you'd ever experienced. Maybe it was because you didn't set it. For people like you, setting alarm clocks is really setting something off.

"All set!" She hasn't really changed, only added a little makeup. Of course, this is when the Valium first hits. But not so much that she can notice.

"Okay."

"Don't you want to take a flannel shirt or something?" This question makes you feel as though she just met you. She knows better.

You don't answer her. When all of the lights are out, you walk outside, with her leading the way. She goes toward your truck and you head to the Rabbit. "You want me to drive?" she asks.

"Please." Across the open field you see that there is more light than when you were out there. That's because the moon is fuller and you're used to staring at that field by now. It is like your own personal outdoor darkroom, where your eyes adjust without even a blink.

You get into the passenger's seat of the tiny car. She has the radio on some country station; someone you can't stand is on. There are so many of them now that you can't tell radio country singers apart. But you are feeling finely fucked up and though it's dark, you pull down the sun visor, only for the mirror so you can see the green grass in the field behind you. "Why are you doing that?" Gina demands to know.

"I want to see back there."

"Back where? There's nothing back there but grass."

"I know."

"Then why?" She shuts the visor. "You're nuts. You can't even see out there it's so dark."

"I can see." Luckily a George Strait song comes on.

"Mama is already talking about you. How she can't wait to see you."

"I can see," you tell her. "I can see back there." You pull down the blinder again and open the window. "I can see all the way back."

"Crazy." She says it lowly. You know that she'll forever deny muttering these strong soft words. "But you know what I heard, is that the Tootles bought it and they are going to build a big ranch there." You can't imagine your leaky trailer facing a mansion.

You are high. "Where were you the other night?" You can't believe you've asked her this. As far as the score goes, she's winning by your dozen nights of no-shows.

You are both sitting there, and she's not backing the old car up. She looks at you and touches you somewhere near your right cheekbone. "I was away."

Because you understand how impossible it is to answer questions like this on the spot, you don't force an answer. "I don't want to go to your mother's."

"I know."

You open your door and get out, knowing now that you're not going. After your door is shut, you walk up those rotting steps to the front door, fumbling for keys. Separation?

Zachary was eighteen and he went to the First Baptist Church because he thought the preacher was sexy. He was built like a linebacker and his voice boomed out, making Zachary shiver at times. He was a former Petulia High football superstar. And just returning from Bible College, he's taken over his father's church. Word had it that he passed up a professional football contract to spread the word of the Lord. Zachary knew this was mostly a lie.

He rarely even listened to the words. Instead, he would sit in the back row, not caring what the preacher was saying. Not believing a word of it, knowing better. Knowing it was all a lie. Knowing what had begun to happen on weekday afternoons when the preacher was there alone.

During his baptism, when he felt the preacher's hands, he knew that he was onto something. He knew the two of them were more alike than anybody else in church knew. This was before too many chemicals and alcohol, before too many hard years of survival. These afternoons were his drug.

The preacher would usually lock the church, though Zachary was sure somebody else must have had a key. The preacher must have seen it in him, because the first time it happened, he simply asked, "Why don't you stop by after your class?"

Zachary arrived on a Monday at 4 p.m. And this time, with the doors locked and the only light coming through the multicolored stained glass and lighting up the room like a peaceful nightclub, this time the preacher didn't mention Bibles; he simply said, "Come here."

And Zachary went. Being in his arms was like finally being accepted by the football players at school, like being part of the breed, even if he was a powerful man in the community. The preacher held him for the longest time. "I've been watching you," he said.

Zachary had heard all about preachers molesting children, but this was different. Zachary was now an adult. And he wanted it.

Across the pew where people had cried and prayed the night before, they tore off their clothes in a frenzy. Each of them as excited as the other.

Zachary was nervous as he was placed across the rough gray carpet near the pulpit, feeling like some sacrificial lamb, like he was part of some extremely mundane, yet exciting event. And it was rough, and the preacher's size was suddenly *a painful asset. But he bit down on his lip until he bled. The preacher went so deep into him. He'd never felt sensations like these before, the flushness, the sweat, the cooling off, the loss of everything except pleasure.*

He felt the preacher bite down on the back of his neck. Then it happened like when he jerked off, cum went all over the place and he felt the preacher pull back for just a second, then let go inside of him.

On that Monday, even when the pain was forgotten, there was still blood from his lip on the carpet. The door opened. The preacher's wife entered the church, all smiles as they had just gotten their clothes on.

"We're in prayer," the preacher said. The woman left them and went into a room in the back of the church.

Now that the pleasure was over, Zachary began to worry. "Am I going to die, now? We didn't use a condom."

"No, kid. You're gonna live a long life."

They scurried around trying to clean the cum and blood. "Am I going to Hell?"

"You're a concerned one. Don't worry. You are going to Heaven."

This left Zachary confused. In fact, from that moment on, he was sure he was going to die and go to Hell.

9

Ten minutes is how long it has been since she drove away. You are standing by the bedroom window, wishing the music would start like it had that night, how that night now seems like important history. The memories are still fresh. The way you stained your clothes, the way the sun exposed itself so early. It felt to you like it had been one of those moments that could have happened in any place, in any century. But you had to be there.

You imagine where Gina has gone. You wonder if she has her secret bars and what men she finds attractive. You are curious, but not angry that she is gone. In fact, her leaving gives you the ultimate opportunity to escape, too. Now you can go out and haunt the town with a face that some consider beautiful, feeling all along like you are flawed because of your craziness. But the pills are running low and you don't want to wake up in a stranger's bed again, no matter how good his shower is. But you do think about getting naked and moving about the thinly curtained room, daring any highway passerby to say a word.

Shedding. First your sneakers, then your T-shirt. You don't touch yourself often enough. You slip the zipper down, loving the sound. Your pants feel good sliding down your legs, good like blue flannel. You rub your still-socked feet against each other. Like boots against boots. And you dream of khakied younger men taking you, teaching you how to love after years of settling for less.

Your cock feels good in your hands. Full of veins, going from pink to dark red, then back again. If doing this is crazy, then you are. Because with every stroke, you are getting closer to those imaginary persons. You are getting closer to fucking people you don't even know. People you've maybe seen at the bar, or those who've offered you Coca-Cola in their single-room apartments.

Alternating between fast and slow, that's how you do it. Then you turn onto your right side toward the mirror on the wall, not minding seeing yourself at the moment. And for this brief time, though you know it will pass like the night, for these five minutes you feel beautiful. Maybe it is because someone at the bar days ago had said you were, maybe it was the music you are sure you heard burning in the field that night. Or maybe it is simply watching your hand beat harder. Faster.

Explosions. In-country, it was noisy and deadly. But here, alone, you will be the only one to shoot. It has been so long, that you blast far, with some of the cum hitting the mirror and beginning a slow drip down.

You stand and go to the mirror, naked like that. While it isn't as good as the music or a fresh bottle of pills, coming leaves you feeling alive.

Half an hour later, Gina's car is pulling into the yard. And you stand there, a little cum still dripping from your cock. You don't move, just wonder if you've dreamed recent things like hovering in the air, hearing opera in the field, feeling beautiful for a few moments.

"Still here?" It is Gina.

"Yeah." You can feel her undressing. "Where did you go?"

"I just rode around and around. I was bored. I feel better now."

You hear her peeing in the bathroom. Next she will put on her nightshirt and walk back into the bedroom.

"There was music," you finally say.

"What?" She is in and out of the bathroom, brushing her teeth in her hot pink nightshirt.

"Music."

"What?" You hear her voice rising.

"Music," you repeat. "From out there," you say pointing to the field.

"You're crazy." She walks over to the window where you are pointing. "There's nothing out there." Gina looks wide awake as she climbs beneath the light-blue sheet.

"Not tonight. But the night that you were gone, there was music coming from out there.

"It wasn't suppose to turn out like this," you say. "When I came back, it was all suppose to fall into place."

"I know. Gary, will you just come to bed?"

There is nothing else for you to do, so you do what she asks.

Facing the mirror, you pull her close, nothing like your LSU days, but definitely tighter than last week. Her nightshirt feels too good to have come from Wal-Mart. She turns off the lamp which always breeds silence. You lie there, holding her close but letting a part of yourself move away at the same time.

When the wind that night blows the curtains in just the right way, and the moon moves slowly or a vehicle passes quickly, you stare at your reflection in the mirror. You no longer feel at all attractive. You think about all of the things that Gina and you have said this night. In that cheap mirror, all you see is the reflection of your newly released cum, some of it in short complete lines fully formed. Crazy white blood.

10

You don't even look at the mirror the next day, wondering if Gina will be impressed or hurt that none of the mirrored stains were for her. You think several times about cleaning it, but of course you don't. And you make another mistake. You are on Somas at work. You've always been able to handle your intake at work. But for some reason, this day, though you only took three, you are flying above the mansion you're building. Your co-workers, they talk to you and you talk back, not at all sure if you're making any sense.

This house that you're working on is going to be beautiful. You wonder if the people who'll reside there will be like that, too. It's probably going to be lived in by some doctor or lawyer. Nailing away, this day, your fingers are safe. They don't get smashed once by your hammer, like they do many other days.

It's strange how when you're not really thinking about the work, you make fewer mistakes, how your thumbs are safer. How by not thinking about what you're doing, you get it done much more efficiently. At least it feels that way. And if it's not true, no one around you has told you. Maybe because of the Somas, you don't wonder if you're totally nailing the wrong way. You wonder if it's just something about the pounding that keeps you going. Maybe if you were the foreman, you'd accidentally build the wrong house on purpose. This thought is enthralling. If you could just build the house your way, for you, even though you know that you'll never live here, it would give you a thrill. Higher than any pills could ever take you.

Even though the other people you are working with, including your boss, Richard, drink a lot of beer, smoke tons of pot, and keep the radio cranked to the classic rock station, they seem oblivious to your fucked-upness. It has always interested you that when you really think you're far out there, nobody notices. And yet when you're just a little high, someone will immediately call you on it. When you make a scene, sometimes you have no idea, until someone tells you later. And when you behave, it's like you expect everyone to see you as a wreck. The pot-smokers to you are like those people who have a slice of cake and say they are stoned from a sugar rush. You know there's a big difference between pot-smoking beer men and people like you. It's like they've never done real drugs. You wish that you were like them.

Sawing is one thing that you hate to do. Though it's part of your job, you avoid it today. Once again, you're afraid you'll do something strange, like cut the wood the way you want and not the way the doctor or lawyer wants it. You stick to the menial work, nailing away, floating above the platform where you are standing, but always come back down.

For a while, you pretend that you are building this house for you and Gina but are interrupted by Richard. "Gary!" It's your boss. You're busted. He's been beyond sugar, and you're sure that he can tell you're trashed.

You climb down the platform. And he's standing there, being Richard, but redder than usual. Next to him is a guy who doesn't look that different from Richard, but probably has more tattoos. You don't care to see either of them without clothes, but you're sure that the other one has more interesting scars because he's got several earrings. Soma thoughts.

"Say, Gary, can you show Jimmy here how to use the new saw?"

All you do is nod. This new guy will not last, as he's one of those just-out-of-prison types, trying too hard. These types of first-timers work out only if they've worked other jobs after the penitentiary.

"Good," says Richard, patting you on your back, not realizing he could have knocked you right down.

"How do you use this thing?" Jimmy asks.

"You take it and you cut wood with it."

"No fuck, but how do you get it to work the right way?"

The saw is there on a table, but neither of you is eager to touch it. "What were you in for?"

"Armed robbery, but..."

"But you were framed." You finish his statement, because they all start out this way.

"No. And for drunk driving. Now what about the saw?"

You look at him straight in the eyes, which seem really big on him, even though he's rather red from the sun. Maybe it's because they're blue and the rest of him is almost ultra-ruby.

"You just take that saw there and you cut. Anything you want. Everything you want. Even the parts that are already put together. Just cut away." Not only can you not believe that you're saying this to him, but that he is actually listening.

"What?"

"That's what this new saw is for. No people, but you can just cut away on whatever you want."

"Really?" He believes you.

You walk away, and over to Richard. "I don't feel well, man," you say. "Can I leave? I really can't stay here until the sun goes down."

"But the house has to be finished before December."

It's not like you don't know this already. "I have to go."

"Well, did you show him how to use the new saw?"

"Yeah."

"Go ahead then."

You know that he is pissed off and will explode at you later over something smaller just for leaving an hour early.

You take off your tool belt and begin to load things into the toolbox Gina bought you the Christmas before John Lennon was shot. You look at Jimmy, who is looking at the saw. You wonder what he'll do with it.

Before you leave, after you've waved goodbye to your co-workers, you walk through the sawdust that you always smell like and then over to Richard. He's annoyed. His anger has grown. But at least he listens, though he doesn't look directly at you.

"Richard?"

"What?"

"Remember the other day?"

"What other day?"

"When I fell."

"Oh, fuck, man. Don't tell me that you hurt yourself or something."

"No."

"What then? We're building a house here. What about you falling?"

"How long was I in the air?"

"What?"

"How long did I hang there, before I landed?"

"I don't know. As long as it took you to land, I guess."

"So it was quick. A quick fall."

"Yes, very quick." He looks at you as if he can't completely see you, squinting as though you are a fading object he's trying to completely take in. "Gary, just go home."

As you load the toolbox into the truck, you want to go back and argue with him. You know that you were in the air for a long time. You want to ask the others, but you're afraid they'd probably say the same thing. As you pull away, you hear a saw, and you are sure it's the new guy. In the distance, you still hear the saws roaring, the nails being driven into the wood. The sawdust follows you up the road. You wonder if the new guy took you seriously, and almost hope that he did. After all, he had that crazy amazing look in his eyes. Art.

11

She has insisted on coming here. To the Catfish Shack. It's full and there is a half-hour wait. She likes it because of the $9.95 buffet. You look around the place and can't believe that this place is full of nothing but families of mostly five or more, and that Gina is willing to wait so long. All of the booths are blue and the waitresses wear the same light-blue uniforms. But not like the curtains in your bedroom; bad blue like it's a shade out of time. Either several decades back or something from *The Jetsons*.

When you are finally seated, she immediately orders the waitress to bring her a large iced tea. She says that this place has the best iced tea in town, and though you always drink beer here, you believe her. There is something different about her tonight, you think. She seems to be nervous, as though she is the one on the verge of some sort of mental crisis. Then again, it's always like this here. You never feel comfortable in a place full of people gorging themselves on fried food, talking so loud that the waitresses must lose their voices from having to yell when they ask the customers what it is they would like.

You are wondering about Richard and just how angry he'll be that you left work early. It's the guilt that's setting in. But maybe, like the memory of shooting an Asian man somewhere between the eyes, it will only return sometimes.

You both order the buffet, of course. Not because you want it, but because Gina always insists that it's the best deal, and that it's the reason people eat here in the first place. So there's that ordeal and you're running out of pills, but still you take your last two Valium, just to deal with the mob at the buffet line. These people are really excited about the hush puppies and shrimp. If you could get excited about these things like them, your life would be so much easier.

After you're both seated, you watch as she drenches much of her food in ketchup. You stare at the redness on her plate and can't believe that she can eat it like that. Ketchup is one thing that you don't ever bother with. You can't.

"Gary, have you heard?" she asks, finally breaking the silence between the two of you.

"What?"

She says it again, louder, thinking that you didn't hear her, when in fact, you didn't understand.

"About what?"

You can tell that this is not easy for her to say. You know it isn't, because she stirs her iced tea slowly and the ice is going to melt before she drinks very much of it at all. The glass may even overflow. You see that she's already spilled some of the ketchup on the table.

"It's Will. He's dead." You want more of something, more information. He's the only friend that you ever had over for dinner. The only person Gina approved of. The only one you could shake hands with in a dirty bathroom and come out feeling cleaner than you had when you'd entered. Your food is sitting in front of you and you're not even touching it. You are so glad that on Monday you can get your prescriptions refilled. All of the noise in the restaurant has stopped for you. So you stare at Gina: in shock that she can tell you such things while ketchup is hanging from below her lower lip. And awed by the fact that somebody just like you has died.

"How? I just saw him the other night. How?"

She is still stirring the tea. It's sloshing all around.

It takes forever for her to speak, and you are not sure if she's even going to tell you the rest. It's as if she wants to savor the events of Will's demise, like she's almost going to keep it a secret. "He was just a man, Gary. It happens to all of us." She is eating away at her food, finally drinking her tea.

"You're right," you say, feeling choked about the end of this whole secret life you had just learned that you and Will separately shared. You don't say anything else.

She looks relieved now, less tense, more relaxed, like when she is at home. The pressure is off her and it's on you, only because she was the one brave enough to speak the words. "What about him?" you ask. You are angry now. And the noise from the restaurant returns. Somehow you are choking, though there is nothing in your mouth but saliva, which is not going down the right way when you swallow.

"Oh, well he didn't show up to work the night shift at the jail. And then, he just did the most unbelievable thing. I can't believe how little you know about what goes on around here, Gary. I was sure that you would have heard about it about by now. I surely didn't want to have to tell you."

"I don't care what goes on around here. But what happened to Will?"

"He killed himself. He jumped from the top of the Wal-Mart into that big concrete parking lot. People were there and they tried to get him to come down, but he didn't. They say he just raised his arms a little, like a bird, and dived. Can you believe that?" You push your plate back while she eats away.

"Yes," you say, "I can believe it." You think of Zachary, of how he could also float from the top of a Wal-Mart, looking like an angel. He keeps coming to mind, this young boy, and you can't stop it, because like everything else that haunts you, you don't know what triggers you to think of him.

The whole restaurant is still packed, and you think about when you saw Will in the bathroom and how if there was anybody that hated that store more than you it was probably him. "I have to go."

"What? Oh, Gary, you're out of your mind. Let's just finish eating. I didn't know that you were going to take it so hard. Gary, you'll be fine. Just wait for me."

"It's not you!" you finally say. "I just have to leave here right now. Why am I here with you in the first place? I should have been on that roof with him. I don't want this fucking shitty food covered in blood. Or to sit in a place where I hear about an old friend dying. Why didn't you tell me about him sooner?"

"Holy shit!" She seems to choke on her words and food at the same time. This is what happens when she gets angry. "So you're more upset about him dying than Lula leaving or the fact that you take pills like they're harmless candy?" She coughs, trying to catch her breath, on the verge of saying something that she needs to get out.

But you beat her to the punch. "I don't know what I'm upset about, but I just want to get the fuck out of here. There are fields out there with music and a whole fucking world and I'm just as tired of this whole rat-trap of pain as you are." You take thirty dollars out of your shirt pocket and throw it on the dirty table. "I'm walking home."

"It's two miles!"

"I've walked a lot farther than that," you remind her.

"Then just go," she says quietly. "You're causing a scene."

People are staring, and you don't care. You want them to see the end of this movie you two are starring in. So you yell. "Get me the fuck outta here!" Pushing past people as you walk away, you feel as wasted as your life.

There are cops scattered around outside to keep the teenagers in line on this Friday night, so they don't pay you much attention as you walk down the back of the strip mall, then back toward the highway. As you pass the restaurant, you see Gina sitting there, her reflection in the mirror, looking radiantly ashamed that your friend, who you never spent enough time with, has crumbled to small-town legendary status.

Fairly sober for a change, you feel the sprinkles of rain and begin to circle the parking lot. It's as though you're playing spin the invisible bottle, hoping that something will ultimately point you in a direction that you will damply follow. You feel yourself getting wetter and the night growing too dark to follow any path, except where your feet take you.

12

You begin to walk up the highway and then something takes over. Night watch. After a few minutes, you stop caring if you are headed in the right direction. Home. You sit down on the side of the highway, realizing that you are indeed headed toward home. For the first time in ages, you feel like walking down the center of the highway. So that's what you do. Not because you want the cars to hit you, or the tropical winds and rain to blow you away. But because Will dove to his death, all covered in colorful marks, probably feeling all along that he was the only bird of that species. And you let the cars swerve in the storm, most of them just barely missing you. The horns make you shake, but don't influence you to move. When a car passes on each side of you at once, you are sure that you can fit between them. After all, you know you were the one it was supposed to have happened to.

Until Will, you thought that soldiers dying were a thing of your past. You hear cars swerving behind you. Breaks squeal. Lights surround you. And as you keep walking you know that battles have become a thing of nostalgic news specials. Wars are a thing of the past. Then you fall to your knees after about a mile of drenching rain. This newly forming river runs deep. Swimming never felt so good. You want to make it home and spin around until you can begin your own battle, can find a way to stop stumbling around so much. That's what cuts you down.

A truck comes toward you and you swear that you stand there for the longest time, at least long enough for it to hit you. But the lights disappear and when you turn around it's as though the truck never even existed. Then you look up a bit, through the subsiding rain, and you see all eighteen wheels of it, floating above the surface. You watch in amazement, but caught off guard, you slip and find yourself in the deep ditch. Swamps. You reach for your machete, then your gun, and when you realize that you don't have either one, you stay silent.

They are around you, as you find yourself drowning with the alligators, dreaming of some R&R. You want them to kill you. Now. Drowning seems to hurt even more than being shot. But there are no guns, only red strobe lights. This is the enemy, and none of them looks any different from the men at the grocery or bank. Their eyes are not slanted. Right now, this is your war. And since you can't fight back, you take your chances by moving through the rising water, hoping that they will shoot you in the back of the neck. So that later, someone might be there to touch your bones the way you touched the bones of men so long ago.

You wish that you could rise up like the big truck did and peacefully ascend. Instead you swim on, wondering how water can fall so fast. And while you hear a few voices from the life that was once yours, you know that this war is one that you can single-handedly win. The cops are nowhere around now; the house can't be much farther. The last thing that you remember doing is reaching for your walkie-talkie, then realizing that you don't actually have one. You are almost home by now. Safety awaits you there.

When you have stopped this marathon of silent running, when you have collapsed somewhere on grass so wet that it seems like a million harmless worms await your restful sleep on top of them. You find yourself curled into a ball on top of all of the wetness. Then the lightning hits, surprising you at how long it lasts, at how it probably wishes to be as permanent as the lost moon. Then the thunder, which you knew all along would follow, enters your ears, a boom you've never heard before in exactly this tone. It feels like the loudest boom you've ever heard. Even louder than when there was fire in the villages with the Vietnamese civilians praying for rain.

This thunder that races through your ears causes you to tremble—a seizure, not a medical one, but a seizure of nervousness sets in and causes you to turn over and look at the sky. You lie there all spread out, arms and legs outstretched. The sky has put a leash on the rain. And now it's a mixture of fast-moving black clouds and night gray. The moon is somewhere, trying its best not to stand you up.

On that ground, once the gray black sky and crescent moon have all become a blur, you close your eyes. And sometime during the night, when the world and you are finally separate, the dream begins. In it, you see these ten or twelve eagles on the ground. You try to count them, but can't get the number exactly right. There is a stadium in this dream, like the one at LSU. And the stadium is full; it's like a graduation or some event that you have always tried never to think about. In this dream, you see your parents in the audience waving, looking proud. But there are no students or football players on the field, only these eagles. And you watch as they begin to fly up. There is some opera in the background, and the birds take off in front of a cheering crowd.

You are invisible in this dream, only watching the birds and the excited spectators. But before the birds get too far into the air, they begin to burn, and this surprises you, but it's not terrifying, not even for the people watching. This is what they've come to see. Destiny. And the birds burn their way to the ground to a cheering crowd. Your invisible self searches carefully for your parents, but you can't find them anymore. This is a dream that feels good even though you wonder how the birds caught fire while on their way up.

13

You awake wet and muddy, glad that it's Saturday so you don't have to work. You feel as though you've slept twice as long as you actually have, refreshed and thrilled that you have not completely missed the sunrise. It's a bright dark orange already, but distant. It reminds you of the sun of the war. It was hot and red over there.

In your last days there, your ability to separate the sun and actual fire became difficult. Red-hot. You hate the way the sunrise always seems so much swifter than its setting. When you have to work, you barely notice it. But right now, you have the time to watch the day begin.

You shake yourself, and feel heavy, weighed down by the water. You look out across the field and wonder whatever happened to the family that lived here years ago, in a house that caught fire one night and burned to the ground, ultimately destroying an entire corn crop. Taking everything except the scarecrow, which was once a strong presence in a place so lacking in real souls. Charred, that old scarecrow is a real scene-stealer. You feel that it still watches over the desolate field alone. Probably wondering where everyone has gone, longing for the yellow corn wrapped in silk but starving for its worms.

When you stand, you are reminded of the eagle dream, surprised that you still remember it, hoping that it doesn't slip away from you like most of your dreams usually do. This is a dream that you don't want turning into a forgotten memory.

The music has begun again. The same stuff. And you are closer to it than you have ever been. It's clearer now, the voice piercing yet peaceful like the thunder from the night before.

Your ears search the field, hoping that it will lead

your eyes to the sound. When the music finally stops, you finally see him. Maybe twenty yards away, as he rises, stretches, and in what seems to be a raincoat, he picks up a boombox and walks through the pale morning. You wonder what other person would be out here in a drenched state like you. But when he turns his back to walk away, a skinny frame disappearing into the new day, you realize who it is. It is because of the way he walks, a little hunched over, the same way he moved when he left you in his apartment a week ago. Disappearance times two. Reappearance. This Zachary sighting leaves you with hope and complete loneliness.

You stand and walk across the highway, squinting your eyes, your clothes weighing more than you. So it's a long haul. You imagine what Gina will be like. You want to tell her about the way that you dream, but you know that she never understands your dreams like you do. Then you think of the boy in the field. You are all full of mud, wondering what you must look like, yet trying to focus on the dream. You don't want the images that rocked you gently as you slept to disappear. You want them to remain whole, instead of coming to you in bits and pieces of sky and fire, the way that so many of your dreams do.

You open the screen door, dreading Gina's inevitable explosion. You want to be quiet so she will keep sleeping. She will never understand the greatness of last night's experience. Selfishness.

You shut the front door as quietly as you've ever done anything. Fear.

Inside, you stare at your reflection in the living-room mirror. Your hair is caked in wet dirt, your face only halfway visible through the dark mud. You wonder if the skinny boy is as muddy as you and why he was in the field.

You tiptoe through the house, searching for a bottle of something to drink. Your eyes become lightbulbs when you discover a bottle of vodka in the kitchen cabinet. You turn the bottle up and drink, wondering where the skinny boy went. Thirst.

You are too dirty to sit; there is already mud on the carpet. So you continue to stand, looking out the window above the kitchen sink, wanting to catch a glimpse of him out there again. You think you hear Gina move, so you just continue to stand there, feeling the vodka bringing you into today, giving you a needed punch. Awakenings.

The phone begins to ring and though you don't answer it, you are surprised that Gina doesn't either. She's never been a call-screener. You hear the machine pick up and walk to the bedroom which looks just like it did the night before when you left to go out to dinner. Whoever has called hangs up without uttering a word. Gina isn't there, and the bed is made in that tight way that only she can make it. You know that she didn't come home last night either. It's as though you can tell just by looking at the carpet that nobody has walked across it since before the disastrous dinner. She's disappeared a few times before when you've pushed her too far with your midnight rambling. Usually she goes to her mother's house to let the craziness subside. You want to fall onto the bed and paint a muddy picture of the night before on the sheets. You want to have the dream again and feel the eagles explode. Instead you head to the bathroom with the bottle of vodka, knowing that a bath is necessary, knowing that Gina will return. And knowing that even when the mud is washed off of you, it will still be there. Mud, you learned in the war, is like permanent makeup to those who wear it for long periods of time. You hear an explosion in the distance and begin to slowly undress in front of the mirror. All made up and no place to go.

Zachary was twelve when his father's heart gave out, just like that. It was the time of year when Mississippi always turned orange and chilly. The county fair was set to start the following day. He wondered where the people from the fair went when they left towns like Petulia. And he wondered why his father would never return from work. It was shortly after the departure of his father that he began to sit in the field alone, wondering if his mother was really going to be okay, wondering if he was also going to die.

In the field where he played as a child, he had recurring fantasies about his father. In one of them, his father had run off with another woman. In another, his father had been kidnapped and would survive, eventually returning a hero of some sort.

On one of these evenings, when his mother was sleeping and his sister was out on a date, he ventured out past the trailer to Mr. Watts' cornfield. When he was younger, sometimes Mr. Watts would let him ride on his tractor with him. Looking somewhat broken in his overalls, he'd tell stories of the Second World War. Zachary saw the liberation of Buchenwald in the black and red colors that Mr. Watts painted with his words.

But on this particular fall evening, Mr. Watts wasn't around. It was only Zachary in that open field. Him and that scarecrow Mr. Watts had made with healthy straw and bluejean and terry-cloth rags. He promised himself that when he got older he would build his own. With his transistor radio flooding the field with Freddy Fender, he watched the straw rags blow in the wind. He was sitting near the scarecrow, facing it. He looked at the scarf tied around the top of it, its eyes drawn on with a black marker. Those mismatched eyes seemed to be staring directly into the house where he lived. He turned to look at the trailer, knowing that once that trailer fell apart, there would be a new one put there. That's how things worked in families like these. But the strange thing was that while Zachary could only see the outside walls of the green-and-white trailer, the scarecrow seemed to be able to see right through them.

A Scarecrow's Bible

When the night grew darker, he began to feel a little afraid of the scarecrow. Not because he thought that he could move and attack him or anything. But because he knew that not only could the scarecrow see what was happening in the house this day, he could see what was going to happen in days to come.

On these nights, after he went back inside, with his mother sleeping her life away, his sister making out with her cute boyfriend on the ugly, green couch, he'd go to his room and not feel part of anything at all. He'd think at these times about the back door and how he had opened it years ago to the wrong person at the wrong time. That's what led him to do it. A part of him that had never felt so heated was unleashed.

In his room, where his Madonna poster hung alongside Morrissey, where his typewriter with a half-typed page sat alone on his sturdy desk, he lit a candle. And while the rest of the family was sleeping, in their own worlds, he slowly took his long thin fingers and tilted the candle in just the right way so that it would set fire to the paper, then to his curtains.

That night he burned their house down. And because he never really felt that it was his house, he never felt guilty. In fact, even years later, he thought that maybe he did the right thing. After they had moved into another sad trailer, his mother stopped sleeping all of the time, and they had a new couch for his sister and boyfriend to make out on.

Even though he admitted doing it, they didn't send him away for it. They didn't have to. He was already farther away from the rest of the town than any of them could ever imagine.

14

You are sitting drowsily in the white bathtub when she walks in. You don't turn to look at her. You hear her sandals sliding across the linoleum floor as she exits the room. "It seems strange with Lula gone, doesn't it?" you ask. She must not hear you because there is no reply. So you shift in the muddy water, which is reminding you of the Mississippi. You haven't been this dirty since the war. You pretend for a moment that it is the Mississippi and that a current is about to draw you under. When you get muddy like this, a shower must follow. But you can't take a shower without thinking of Zachary.

The vodka bottle, empty, floats in the water like a tugboat. It pushes against your leg, but you can't be moved. The shower walls are lined with pastel tiles. They are falling off. You want to remove some of them yourself. There's something about stripping away the covering of the wall one piece at a time that makes you forget how lonely a muddy swim in a minuscule bathtub can be.

Then she returns and starts throwing things from the medicine cabinet into a small bag. Things, like cheap soap and hair spray, that those who love Wal-Mart cannot live without. You grip the vodka bottle as though you can drink the air from it and still get drunk. You're holding the bottle like the hand of a dying friend. It's the same way you'd hold Gina's if only she'd let you.

"Gina," you call out. "What's going on with you? What the fuck's going on?"

"I'm leaving you," she says as she comes to the doorway.

"You're leaving?"

She answers again and again by zipping suitcases and throwing things into boxes. As you listen to these scary sounds, you pull one of the loose tiles from the wall. "Who is it? Did you find someone else?"

This gets her back into the bathroom where she looks at her reflection in the mirror like she's falling in love with herself. "Yes." She is crying.

"Who is he?"

"Eddie."

"The cop?"

"There are some good cops, Gary. You can't knock them all. And this way you can start over again, too." She seems like she is going to come over and touch you somewhere, anywhere. "Have you seen the hair dryer?" she asks.

"Bottom shelf," you tell her as she sees it, grabs it by the handle, and wraps the cord around it before putting it into a small cardboard box.

In your hand you hold the piece of tile, which you squeeze hard enough to distract you from getting out of the tub.

"Don't hate me, Gary."

But you can't help yourself. "A cop?"

"You'll never get it. This love thing." She's searching the bathroom closets and drawers, making sure she didn't forget anything.

"You're right," you tell her. "I never will."

"That water's disgusting. And why do you keep taking tiles from the wall? Pretty soon there won't even be a wall there." She leaves the room as determined as she entered it.

In your Mississippi River, you continue to make yourself breathe. Unfortunately, there is no undertow to take you away. But you are too weighed down by your own shock to rise. This is it. You call out her name a couple of times, but eventually it sinks to nothing more than a whimper. You can't blame her for leaving you. You'd leave you too.

You stand, knowing that if you don't rise now, they

may find you here years from now, dead in a crust of dirt. As the shower water hits you, you are at first shocked, then calm. This is one of those moments in your life when you know that nothing will ever be the same again. It makes you feel like an aging newborn. There is no one to turn to. And holding yourself has become mundane.

As you squeeze the pink, sharp tile harder, and the water hits your face, your palm begins to bleed from the cut it has made. You watch as it drips down into what's left of the muddy water, creating an angry color all around your feet. The vodka bottle is banging against the side of the tub as you wash. And you are hoping that when you step out, that you'll be in a different place from where you were when you first ran your bath water. A place that will feel as fresh as the cut in the palm of your right hand.

15

Her packing brings a load of unpleasant noises. You listen, trying not to, as she alternately talks to you and herself in opposing tones that make no sense. Any person who walked in on this scene would think that she would be angry, but you know that she is not. Instead she's just keeping herself going. She's saying things like, "Yes, I'll need this," or "I'll give this to the Salvation Army." Maybe she's trying to convince herself, more than you, that she is actually going. You know that she actually is. In the past, this would have all ended with her waiting for you to beg her to stay. And that's what you always did back then. Today, she races around the house, all rushed like she wouldn't even listen to you even if you were on your hands and knees, yelling prayers.

You let her move through this marathon. If you weren't so annoyed by your cut hand and so comfortable in the recliner, you would have timed her to see if her finishing time would be as fast as Lula's. You wonder what things she will take that you'll miss. You can't feel your right hand the way you should be able to, but you feel it a lot more than the rest of your body. Sobriety has set in. Coming down.

"This is a dream. This is a fucking long dream that won't quit," you say to her as she comes into the living room with some hangered clothes and tosses them on the couch. "What all are you going to take?"

"Just some pictures. But that's it. Eddie has everything else. He's got that big house on Williams Road."

Now that she's said this, you wish that she would take everything. How nice it could be to roam through an empty trailer after a night out, making as much noise as you want. It could be lovely to come home without any furniture to fall into. As you'd stagger against the air, the floor would welcome you. It has never pushed you away, no matter how many times you've lain on it. But this thought of an empty palace of poverty is cut short when she says, "I don't need any of the furniture."

"It doesn't matter."

"Don't pout, Gary."

"I thought that maybe I had a little bit of a right to look somber."

"You always look somber." She says this as she moves around the house. "But I do want the encyclopedias, that's the only other thing. And the cuckoo clock. I want the fish tank, but it's too much of a hassle."

You want to remind her that only moments ago she said that she didn't want anything. But you let her go on, seeing how she keeps slowing to check out the living room. She's looking less beautiful now, all sweaty and pale from the fatigue of moving even the smallest things. She goes to the encyclopedia shelf where she scans it. "One of these is missing. An 'A' volume."

"It's under the couch. Remember, we put it under there to balance it off?"

"Would you mind raising up the couch?"

You walk over there, knowing you'll have to find another sturdy book or a block of wood from the tool-shed to level it off. Maybe you can use some of the *TV Guide*s. After she's pulled the book out, she begins to put the encyclopedias in a cardboard box. She's gotten the box from the Tastee-Freez, and it looks sturdy enough, but when someone is leaving you, the packing boxes always look like strong coffins.

You sit on the arm of the couch and make it become a balanced piece of uncomfortableness again. It is like sitting in most places during the war. Even when the ground or cot in Vietnam was level, it never seemed balanced. You always found yourself feeling like you were sliding over there, toward enemy fire, or slipping closer to a mine. She drops about four of the encyclopedias into the box. Loudly. You jump and the couch tips to the left. You almost fall. You stand and then sit.

"Sorry," she says, taking the final encyclopedias. She looks at you when she says this and you know she means it, but you can't let it get to you.

You are sitting there, the slight shaking subsiding. And you realize that your position has left you feeling all spread out in an all-over-the-place state. You are taking up the whole couch. She seems to be taken aback when you start laughing. "Fucking ridiculous," you laugh on.

She finally slows her movement and begins to laugh too. Only louder than you. This doesn't surprise you, as you know it's funny how you jumped and nearly fell. And some of the tension seems to get sucked into the laughter and rise until it slips through one of the newly forming holes it the ceiling. She is by you now. And she looks beautiful again. Chameleon housewives. When she sits down, she naturally slides close, right next to you. She needs to be kissed. You hold her with your bandaged hand, wondering what a mess you must seem, knowing that it's all a pretty ridiculous sight. But not to her. You know this because of the way that she is looking at you. And you see her change, like someone dying. You see her life pass before your eyes. And she begins to look younger again. To age gracefully.

Her lips are drier than yours. You think again how she needs to be kissed. You make it a good one, deep, like it is the first time. Re-virginized lips. "Would you," she asks, reaching the top button of your shirt, "love me one time all the way, so I don't have to leave?"

The kiss was what you had craved, but now she wants more as her hand strokes your chest. Down below, you are numb. Like you were once shot there by a woman and therefore can't make it work with them. Friendly fire.

"Come on, after eleven years of never doing it, can't

you just give me this one thing to make me stay?"

"Just a few minutes ago, you were in a big rush to leave."

"Because looking at you makes me want one last amazing touch."

"But you're leaving me."

"I still love you, Gary."

"Me too."

"We'll never hate each other like we're probably supposed to. I know that I get angry, but I still love you. And you still love me, even when I'm in a bad mood."

She sounds like a man to you. It doesn't embarrass you, but you know that her lines are those that men usually utter. You wish you'd said them first.

"Even when you're leaving me?"

She nods. "Even then."

The kiss that ensues is good and you try and keep up with her, but her tongue is so forceful. How can the tongue of someone you love grow so old so fast? You've had enough now.

You push her away as she reaches for your belt. "You look a million years younger when your T-shirt is bleached white and your eyes are blue at the end of the day. I stayed with you for so long because I knew that I'd never find a man who became more beautiful as time passed." She unzips your pants and reaches inside. To age gracefully.

Her hand on your cock feels like a poisonous rub down. Snakes, you once heard as a child, could either melt away in the sun or be choked to death with a single human hand. Disappears.

"I can't." You push her off of you. "I can't."

"I figured," she lets go of you as you stand up and walk toward the bedroom.

"I'm sorry..."

She doesn't say anything else as you walk to the bedroom, where you find that she has taken the sheet off.

Maybe she will clean the place out after all, taking everything. This doesn't stop you from lying down on the rough mattress, wondering what patterns will be imprinted on your flesh when you awake.

16

Stillness is what tears you from the mattress, which you are practically stuck to. The house has never been this quiet, except for maybe yesterday when you sat in the tub after your swim in the mud. But that was different, because before you always knew that eventually Gina would return. Now you know that this stillness isn't going to be broken unless you are the one to do it. That's why when the phone rings, you are not only surprised, but almost afraid to answer it. It makes you jump up from the bed. The room is pretty spare now. Gina took a lot of things. Most of them unimportant, yet things that had been in their places for years. Lonely shelves, lonely walls.

"Hello," you say, surprised that Gina didn't take the phone with her, too.

"Daddy." Lula sounds like she's calling from another country.

"Honey..."

"Daddy," she says again, then again, "Daddy."

Something about the way she says this, the way she repeats it, brings a newness to the word, like nobody has ever been called daddy before. "Lula, how's life in the big city?"

"Good, Daddy. Got a good job bartending. I've never been so happy." Her voice still sounds like hers, but it's got a richness to it that you always wanted to hear from her.

"Where are you staying? Money's okay? Are you eating?"

"Yeah," her voice falls a little. "But I'm trying to diet. I've got everything I need right here in the French Quarter. I'm going to be staying with my friend Chris for a while until I find my own place."

"You sound good, Lula."

"How's Mama?" She asks this, her voice stronger than strong.

"Fine," you lie without guilt. "Just fine."

"Is she here?"

"No."

"How are you, Daddy?"

"Good. Working, you know. A little drinking here and there, but mostly behaving."

"Liar," she laughs.

You laugh back. "Oh, all right, you got me. I haven't been perfect. But I'm good."

"Well, I guess I'll be coming home to visit for a weekend someday soon, Daddy. But you know that's when we make most our money."

"Come soon."

"Or you come here. You and Mama can sleep on the sofa bed."

This strikes you as funny, and you laugh nervously. "Yeah, I guess we could."

"Why are you laughing?"

"Because it's good to hear you, Lula."

"I feel like a new person here, Daddy. Brand new."

"You sound like it. It's good to hear you, Lula."

"Daddy, I gotta go. Tell Mama I love her and to come visit. And you, too. I want to pick up the phone and call you all the time. Just to say nothing."

"So you haven't changed that much."

"No, no, I have. Like right now I've gotta let you go, because I can't run up the phone bill too much."

"Lula?"

"Yeah?"

"Do you remember when you ran the phone bill here up to five hundred dollars with those 900 numbers?"

"Yeah."

You don't want to let her go. You don't care if the phone bill turns out to be five hundred dollars and you have to pay it. Keeping her on the line is like you've never talked on the phone before. Letting go has never been a great skill of yours.

"Daddy, are you all right?"

"Hell, I'm good."

"Great, I'll call you soon."

"Okay, honey."

"I love you, Daddy."

"I love you, too." The words you mean just come out.

"Tell Mama to call me."

"I will."

"Goodbye, Daddy."

"Lula, Lula, goodbye."

Hanging up the phone is like losing some sort of connection to the world. Your only connection. You are happy for her, working at the pub on the corner of Bourbon and St. Anne. You lie back, imprints of the sheetless mattress on your right side. And you are envious and happy for Lula, not just for getting out, but for putting herself in the world in a way that you never had the guts to.

You daydream that you are younger, and then even more young, mixing drinks, dancing wickedly well, seductively, behind a bar where you belong. And in this dream, love comes your way in the forms of beautiful ones. When they wink at you or tip you an extra dollar, it's as though everything you've ever done is all right. You are validated.

When you stop this daydreaming, you find yourself with a bottle of vodka. And reality hits, because you know that you can't go back. You are too old to mix martinis for young boys and dance elegantly. So you drink alone at the kitchen table, knowing that all bottles run out.

Daddy.

17

That night, after you talked to Lula, you drink yourself into the sunset, the curtains blowing through the open windows. It's just past seven and you're completely ready for bed. And you find yourself back in there, feeling like calling in sick tomorrow will be the best thing that you can do. You know you're getting behind in the bills, but things with money always work out. There's always a way to pay next week for tonight. Credit cards, loans from banks that charge 30-percent interest. There's always a way.

You search the bedroom closet for some sheets. You find a tacky pink set and try to put them on the bed, but they don't quite fit, so you sort of spread the fitted one across it. You are tired of the lines the mattress has been making on your body. Even though they disappear after a while, they still leave you feeling beyond old, almost unhuman. So you just lie there against the pink sheets, in the dark, alone like you haven't been in years. In fact, you are alone like you've never been before.

The window is blowing cool air. You know that you can't go on like this for much longer. Open windows, opportunities. Your rut has become deeper. Escape.

You toss and turn, holding nothing but pillows bought five years ago. His and hers. You think about calling Lula, but you remember that she's working. You sit, sobering up. The traffic on the road outside is mixing with the sounds of the new night wind. And you walk over to the window and look out into the nothingness, at the earth that was your bed just a night ago.

In Vietnam, when the sun went down, it was the witching hour. It was the time when you wished for daytimes that lasted forever, but lately you've been preferring the nights. Darkness has become more vivid to you. You love to be in the dark, watching the objects become completely clear. Clearings are all over, but as you stand, you still fight your way a little through the bedroom. Insomnia has set in. Thoughts of tomorrow's refills on prescriptions make it more difficult to sleep.

So you find yourself on the front steps of the trailer. You wonder why you and Gina had gone so far into debt just to pay for this place, the old trailer you'd had was fine, but she just had to have one like her sister's. Things like this really bother you when you think about them. Her sister felt that everybody should own a double-wide trailer situated in a big enough yard for barbecues. Gina always talked about entertaining, but she never did. Then again, how could she? With someone like you wandering around the house, how could anybody plan a party? You know that it was you that prevented them. Now you know that something has ended. Party-givers like you always end up seeming like party-crashers. This is never admired, you know, only pitied.

Had you not seen what death looked like so frequently, so many years ago, you would have sworn that you were gone. Had you not smelled it in Vietnam, you would have been sure that it was all over you now. You pull a light-blue button-down shirt around you. Your boxer shorts aren't very warm, and your bare feet are growing a little cold. You look around outside the trailer, your memory working overtime, and you remember the spot. One of those hiding places you only notice when you're sober.

Across the wet dew you walk and begin to dig mercilessly in the dirt with your hands. You are not far from the steps and just beneath the trailer. At first you think you've found it, then you stand quickly, reaching for the gun that is not there. And you throw the stick that looks so much like a human bone across the highway, closing your eyes, hoping that since it isn't curved, it will not come back. Then you dig a little beside that spot and find them. Half a bottle of Somas you'd hidden from Gina a month ago, the bottle wrapped in a plastic bag. Suddenly you feel alive again.

You swallow two of them straight, one of them melting so much that you feel the need to puke immediately. So you go inside and take a glass of water, and when you go back outside to listen to the mosquitoes, the bitter taste still overwhelms you, but you don't really care. At least you know it will pay off when the white light from the pills hits you. You know this is a problem. The things that are suppose to make you aware, like plenty of sleep, make you disoriented. But downers, like these white pain pills, make you keenly in touch with everything surrounding you.

You lean against the door of the still-unpaid-for trailer. It and the singing mosquitoes are your only companions. You learned long ago that if you don't swat them too much, they sing more beautifully. So their voices rise and soon turn into something spectacular. That same music you've heard before; this time when you see the skinny figure in the distance, you don't get overly excited. Instead, you lie back and listen. You don't even look too much at the beautiful figure in the field, you just take in the music. You want to hear the music again, like the last time when you saw him in the field. And for the first time you think you actually understand some of the words. Not completely, but it makes you get up and go inside. You lie on the empty bed with the wrinkled sheets which you know you'll be wrapped in too tightly by morning. And you let the music flow through the window and put you away, your paws so dirty from digging in the dirt, your eyes heavy with sleep.

18

"So there are voices you hear?" Doctor Wilkes asks in his chilly, dark, blue office with scratchy furniture and obtuse plants.

"No."

This is why you hate coming here, to this therapy. Because they tell you what they want to hear, always expecting you to repeat it back. It's like they're trying to teach you their language. Persuasion.

"But you just said..."

"I was just telling you that I hear music in the fields, not voices. Well yeah, voices, but singing voices."

"And what kind of singing?"

This man who is asking the questions seems like he's really trying to help you. And you know that he is. But unlike you, he went further than two years of LSU and got rich. He is good-looking like a soap-opera doctor, and nothing you can say can top him. Nothing can prove him wrong. You've argued with him before, only trying to get him to believe you. But they always think that you are lying. It's as though they don't have to understand because they think they know the truth the moment you begin to talk.

And it's not a war that you're trying to have here. You're really trying to talk to him, to tell him the truth. But his high cheekbones and the desk photo of his beautiful family at the church function make you feel like you're not sitting at eye level with him. Instead you feel like you're sitting on the floor. So you look up at him. "Now tell me," he pushes, "what does this music sound like?"

"What's it like to be a deacon in the church?" You ask this because you are truly curious to know what it's like to live a life like that. But mostly you want to change the subject.

Doctors like this really think you're much crazier than you are; that's why they ignore questions like this. If these therapists could only step inside of your head for a few moments, they'd not only learn something about you, but they'd learn something about everybody. There are things you could teach people like Doctor Wilkes that they have no idea exist, but you don't know how to say them the right way. He's smarter than you. You could turn his world upside down, if he allowed you to. You could force him to question everything he believed in. But he won't let you get that far. Still, this thought of your knowing some things he doesn't makes you feel like you are back in your chair and not on the floor.

"Gary?"

"Yes?

"The music. Tell me more."

"Well, it comes from the field, and there's a young man out there who plays it."

"I see..." He says this as if it's the most important thing he's ever heard. "So this young man not only shows up in fields at night, he's also a musician."

"No." You stop for a moment, not wanting to explain it, but the doctor stares at you. And you feel obligated to give him more. "He has one of those things, you know, like all the kids have. A box. A jam box, boom blaster, whatever they call 'em."

"So you've not only heard this fellow, but you've seen him as well?"

"Yes."

"What does he look like?"

"Never got a close-up." You are squirming in your chair; the doctor seems to be believing you now. You look dead into his eyes. They are dark. You know this could all be over if he said to you that you were still the same as always. That you'll never exorcize your demons from all those years ago. But with him, you feel like you're not getting rid of any darkness. In fact, it's as though you're meeting with your own personal devil.

"But what about your wife? Does she hear the music? Before she left? Did she hear it?"

"No, but..." You want to tell him how she isn't the type of person who would notice these things.

"So you're the only one hearing and seeing this person. How can you tell he's young?"

By the way he moves."

"How is that?"

You rub your tennis shoes back and forth across the flat carpet, just wanting your pills and to escape.

"How does he move, Gary?"

"Well, he's really tall and skinny, real scrawny, and he just moves slowly, like a determined child, but I know he's twenty-something."

"How can you be sure?"

"Trust me." You don't feel like going into the morning you woke up in Zachary's apartment.

Doctor Wilkes is a lot like what you could have been had you not been over there for so long. "How long were you over there?" you ask him.

"A couple of months, I guess. Not long, nothing like what you went through." His eyes on yours reveal that even his robotic air has its weaknesses. "I was never on duty, just a doctor, like now."

You think that the word "doctor" may be overused and that many times people like Doctor Wilkes push the title to an extreme where it packs less punch. You're not jealous, just disgusted that you and he could have easily had each other's lives. But at the same time, you wouldn't want to be like him, spending your days in an office this clean. He is looking at you more now, and you can actually see yourself in the pupils of his black eyes.

"We don't speak the same language," you finally say.

"What?" He stops writing and puts the clipboard down.

"We don't speak the same language," you say again. "Can I just get my scrips and go?"

"What?"

"We're not on the same wavelength," you explain to him, though he is supposed to be the smart one. "What you say, what I say, it's like we're from two different countries. It's not the same language," you repeat. "You don't know what it was really like over there. You don't know what it's like to really see and hear things in the night that nobody would ever believe. You're on top of the world, Doctor, and I'm still a soldier thinking that one of you here is going to fix me. So it's not the same language. You talk from up there, and I talk up to you. I've got nothing else to say. I just need my pills."

"I do know what it's like," he says. "And I do believe you." And the way he says it lets you know that he really does.

You feel good for a moment, having connected, knowing that someone finally believes what you've said.

"Doctor Wilkes? Do you think I'm crazy?"

"Yes."

You are floored and wait for the laughter, sure that he is joking. But he's not, because he begins to go over your file and writes out your prescriptions. "Anybody who heard those screams in the night, and the sky lighting up, everybody waiting to be blown up, made us all that way." He puts his hand on your shoulder. "I still hear the voices begging me to keep them alive. And just like now, with you, even though you veterans lived longer than some of those boys, I still can't keep everyone alive."

You are silent and take the prescriptions, knowing he doesn't want to give them to you, knowing that if he doesn't you'll be miserable. "Thanks, Doctor."

"You can't come in here once in a while and expect to be saved. It's not church, at least not the kind I believe in. You have to come back and when you get here, you have to talk."

"I know that."

"There was one guy in bed, who was also from Mississippi." The doctor is looking out the window now. "And he had this tube down his throat and he couldn't talk, couldn't say a word, and the nurses would hold his hand until he'd finally pass out."

You are not sure why you are still here. When Doctor Wilkes turns around, you see him wipe his eyes with his sleeve. "You're like that boy. Your throat is fine, but still you can't really talk."

You hold onto your prescriptions. Soma, Valium, and Seconal. And you don't say another word; you squeeze his hand tightly and let go. "See you next time," he says. Maybe the language is the same after all, but you can't speak.

You only came for the prescriptions but are leaving with something else. You know that some men have a way of breaking down that other men just don't know what to do with. That's why you leave, probably seeming cold, but actually you are on fire with the image of what he just told you. Doctor Wilkes is a man who held other people together, standing in the window, falling back and forth in time, just as helpless as you ever were. You think about going back in, but know that maybe, like you, he likes to hurt alone. You walk through the hospital with all of the elevator bells sounding like bombs bursting in foreign air.

Outside the Biloxi hospital, you walk across the highway to the beach where you stare at the muddy Gulf of Mexico. You listen to people honking their car horns as though there is no time left to get anywhere. As though time isn't suppose to stop once in a while.

If the water weren't so murky, you'd wade in it and remember what it was like when your parents took you here as a young boy. Instead, you get bored and don't even wait for the sun to go down. You head for the nearest pharmacy.

By the time you reach your truck, you don't know what you'll do after the pharmacy. You don't want to get too loaded, because that whole promenade is growing old. You want something new. Perhaps because of the doctor, you feel stronger. For the first time in months, you feel like you might be just fine. Sanity rears its head.

19

You drive after that session. It's what you do as the Mississippi day becomes night, and as the therapy turns you into a happily high highway man. You don't know where you want to go. The city would be nice. New Orleans, of course, not a city in Mississippi, because no matter what, the cities in this state are not really cities at all. Instead they are beautifully tranquil places where people feel at home as long as they are not being themselves. You do love Jackson, though, and you even love Petulia, but you wished that they loved you back. As you speed up the interstate, feeling rock solid after just a single Valium, you realize it's not just Mississippi but the entire South, perhaps the entire country, that is like this.

But New Orleans is not the South. Like Florida, it is its own private country, attached to a nation foreign in ways that even desperate tourists must understand. Independence and rebel flags almost make sense at a time like this. It is a unique place that reminds you of the week you spent in Paris when you were a student at LSU. But it's grittier in New Orleans. For you, New Orleans is a Paris scorched by flames, but never burned completely away. The fire left just enough soot and peeling walls to allow the people that belong there to scrape and glide through alcohol-drenched streets and make it their home.

On your way there, you think about the doctor and wonder why you didn't stay and hold his hand. Selfishness isn't going to ruin your drive, though. You turn up the radio and channel-flip until you find something that you've never heard before. But you don't care, because in the New Orleans clubs, the same thing will happen. Preparation.

In the rearview mirror, you see your face. And it's not bad. In fact, you might even look good. Your hand is still cut, but you'll ignore it, hoping that everyone else will, too. And if they don't, you can try and seek Lula out.

Waffle Houses and many Shoney's line the road to your new night out. It's been over two months since you've been to the city. A Wal-Mart billboard sticks out at you, and for a brief moment, you swear it is falling sideways onto the road, ready to crush you and the truck. But after blinking, it still stands erect. You don't want to take that exit. From now on, any time you see a Wal-Mart, it will be as though that one is the one Will jumped from. Once you've seen one of those stores, you've seen them all. So it's like he's jumped from every single Wal-Mart everywhere. And sometimes, when you get carried away, you see him jumping from all of them. From the one in Pascagoula, the one in Slidell, the one in Metairie. In your mind, Will is constantly jumping from a roof, without touching the ground. Maybe in your mind, he always will be.

You channel-flip some more, looking for anything to shake you up, looking for something to get you past the twin span bridges that will lead to your night out. Gina comes to mind, but only when you think about the trailer. So you focus on the field and the city, places so different that they only match in the way they relieve you. They are almost at odds with one another, as you've mentally pitted them against each other, wanting both of these opposite necessities. Magnetic fields, soft concrete.

There is a station playing opera, but you turn it, because it sets you back, moves you in a direction that you don't want to be going in. In fact, you can almost feel the car moving backward as the opera overwhelms the air. The Jeeps in Vietnam felt the same way. Over there it was like rolling back into grass that grew so high and alive that it cut like glass. But the field across from the trailer is not where you want to be tonight. You change the station back to the dance music that you don't even like. But you're preparing yourself, so you don't argue with the night ahead.

When the city comes into view, you begin to think about parking. It's always difficult to find a place to park your car. The garage by Jax Brewery is your best bet.

You want to see something new; you want to see life. And you want to see tonight no matter what it turns out to be, even though it will do nothing but lead to tomorrow. But that is an eternity away.

The lights of the city move closer to you. You take another Valium. Tonight, you will stay in control. You won't let yesterday's disasters block your path. Right now, you are amazing to you. Right now, you want a parking spot and a drink. Old habits die slow deaths. Control.

The city is on you now. You feel the heat and sweat invading the car. Your hand is still healing, your eyes glazed, your gas tank nearly empty. But being you never felt like this. It never felt so good.

There are only a few brief bursts of memories. Of men, a certain man falling over and over again from the Wal-Mart just outside the city. Or the bodies that are piled into the back of the truck that momentarily feels like a Jeep. But they are short memories that you can dispense with rather quickly.

You promise that you'll let yourself hold the hand of your doctor more often, and that you'll have a good time tonight, regardless of its events.

20

You slow down once you get in the bar. Inside, the fog from outside is replaced by cigarette rings and smoke-filled conversations. It is less thick than the fog outside, but still, walking around the bar alone is like cutting the air with each step. You wish that your shoes had daggers at the toe. Anything that keeps the smoke from rising makes your breathing less difficult. Suffocation.

This is the bar where you always come. You don't see Lula anywhere. You wanted her to be working. Downstairs there is this muscled man feeding the crowd drinks that will later get them to say "fuck me" to another person who's also drunk too many of the multicolored drinks.

The crowd is mostly younger than you, and all of the other ones are in groups. Lawyer types, full of excitement, like they've never been out before. Maybe some of them haven't.

There are video screens which you follow around the bar. It's the same music that you've found makes most gay bars feel the same. You finally sit down on a stool. You want to look at the people, and you want them to look at you. But your eyes are directed at the ninety-nine bottles of liquor on the wall. People shove at your shoulders from each side. Attack.

You study them as they move their bodies to the bar and take their drinks. You wonder what they look like, but refuse to see a thing. Selective blindness.

The bartender asks what you're having so quickly, that you say vodka on the rocks because it's the first thing that comes to mind. Memories. The bartender is the only person you have noticed, not because he is extremely good-looking but because he is in control of the drinks.

"Is Lula working?" you yell to him.

"No. Tomorrow night," he says, shaking his head assuredly.

The video screens bore you. There are tons of women and men, clad in leather, singing music which you are sure is bad. This finally leads you to look around.

"Anyone sitting here?" this tall man, the size of a toothpick asks you.

By the time you shake your head, you are nearly finished with your drink. Of course you want another.

"I'm Michael," he says, probably around forty, but looking much older.

You shake his hand and down the rest of your drink. You are a little drunk as you stand and move toward the stairs which lead to another part of the club. Maybe Lula is working upstairs and the bartender just didn't know it. You are still okay on your feet and plan on staying that way. You pay your five bucks and they stamp your hand so you can traipse upstairs to the unknown. Halfway up the stairs, you can hear the music changing. It is always better up here in this place which seems miles higher than the bottom floor. To rise slowly.

Up there, it is packed, with a dance floor full of every type of gay man and woman God ever made. There are hustlers, rich couples looking for a boy or girl, and girls in love with their gay-male friends. These people know where to come to find their family. Home is where the strobe lights are.

You watch them all moving differently, yet in some sort of synchronized way. Of course by now you've ordered another vodka and popped another chalky blue Valium. Leaning against the wall, someone bumps into you with such force that it causes you to spill much of your drink in many directions. You want to be out there, dancing with them, but don't have the guts to go into the pulsing lights alone.

You are high now, drunkenly so. Once, in the army,

there was a party where nobody asked you to dance and yet you got out there and danced alone. Those were things that you could get away with at twenty. Yesterday.

Air would be good, so you walk to the balcony doors, and the cool air hits you in a beautiful way that allows you to fully breathe again. Outside, on the balcony overlooking the city, you see New Orleans split in three. It is a city beyond schizophrenia. Below there are Hurricane drinks and their addicts; above, the sky seeming to ignore the decadence which is in full effect. And across the street is a quiet home with a wrought-iron balcony. Nothing seems to be going on in the house. It's hard for you to imagine that anyone lives there. Except for the few kissers that are scattered around, the balcony has few people. To be kissed on a balcony, beneath a nonjudgmental sky, is something that you haven't felt in a while.

Then, because of the alcohol, you walk around the corner of the building, hoping this side of the balcony has an empty bench. There are two benches. On one, kissers who you are too envious to imagine the love of, make you look away.

But it is the second bench which sobers you up, forcing you to swallow a Valium dry. It is him, Zachary, the boy from the fields. His left nostril is covering a straw sucking softly whatever he has poured onto his wrist. He sort of throws his head back and leans against the brick wall. You're thirsty and think about going back in for a drink. But he could disappear again. So of course, you rush to the bar and order a drink as quickly as you've ever ordered anything.

"Wanna dance?" a handsome man asks. He is wearing the type of sweater and brown shoes that people like him order from those catalogs where everything looks like cool autumn.

"No," you lie, "I'm here with someone."

"Me, too."

"No," you say again, tripping over people as you venture back outside. Before you even turn the corner, you can already sense that he is gone. This is the type of creature you've noticed him to be.

Still he sits, skinnier than ever. Quite pale, almost too white. But it is a rare whiteness that goes beyond junkie-dom. His particular light coloring is just white enough, making it seem like a state of being more than a pale shade. And there is something about his skinniness that has attracted you from the start. Maybe it's because you picture the hardness of his bones through his layers of tattered baggy autumn clothing.

You walk over to him. This is what Valium and vodka allow men like you to do. Bravery of the worst kind. And you sit down beside him. He is wearing a brown flannel shirt and wide-legged jeans, frayed at the bottom. The wind blows a little, and you watch him shiver. You see what the straw has done to him. It's made him float a little away from the balcony. You feel more removed from him, like you're sitting by a stranger on a bus. It's as though he's never seen you before. With your jacket over your T-shirt and your khakis, you feel not only older than he is, but as old as his grandfather.

"Hello," you say, too quietly for a high boy to hear.

But he does. And when he turns to you, you notice how the tiny hoop in his left ear, his minuscule eyes, and small nose, make his face complete. A person with any of these features out of balance at all wouldn't have interested you. But he matches himself in every way, making it nearly impossible not to stare.

Finally, he looks at you. Recognition. "Hi," he smiles and you know it's genuine, because it doesn't fade away. Then he smiles again this time wider, showing his bad teeth, then covering them with his hand. It is a pleasure for the two of you to have defeated this loneliness.

"Remember me?"

"Sure. You are better tonight." While his teeth are nowhere near-perfect, they are white and you can see yourself liking them, licking them as though they are multishaped candy. Sweetness. "You aren't passing out tonight"" he asks you. You watch him watch you take a sip of your drink. "Well, I guess not yet," he adds. "Want some?" he asks, offering you some of the coke in the bag.

You know it will revive you, so you take the straw, do two lines and feel your heart become extremely aware, almost overriding the Valium. Speaking of which, you hand him one.

"I have heard you," you tell him.

He takes the Valium and washes it down with some of your vodka, like it's an oasis. "Heard me?" he wonders.

"In the field. I heard the music..."

He seems embarrassed and looks at the floorboards below. "Sometimes I get bored, and I go out there and wander around."

"Why?" The coke in the back of your throat scares you. You could learn to love this bitter taste.

"Just to remember where I came from I guess. I bring books out there and my music."

"What do you read?"

"Poetry mostly." He suddenly smiles. "I can't believe you are here. I never thought that I'd see you again."

"I saw you in the field. Did you ever see me?"

"No, my eyes are bad. I only like to see what is near me. I thought about getting glasses or contacts, but then I'd have to see the beautiful people when I come to places like this. And besides, I'd really be able to see Petulia's flaws then."

You want to tell him he's beautiful, but he stops you.

"Can you feel the coke?"

"A little. I guess we shouldn't get too fucked up."

He reaches into his shirt pocket and does a line so

quickly that it reveals to you that he does it all the time. You can see him all wired so you take the bag of coke from him and hand him two Valium.

The coke is strong. New Orleans looks dark; it's not going to rain. But it feels like a cemetery night to you.

"We shouldn't get too fucked up," he says as you taste the coke overwhelming the vodka.

You'll need another drink soon. He washes down the pill you give him with what's left of your vodka.

The balcony seems still as you sit alongside this aging boy, this slenderly grown field mouse. When his fingers touch your face, you want to know even more about him. "I think you're beautiful," he says. "And I'm close up."

You sense a kiss, but he leaps up and walks to the wrought-iron balcony.

"Can I get you a drink?" he asks you.

"I was going to get you one."

"Do we even need more?" he asks.

"Yes."

"I guess we might as well get really fucked up tonight," he says, changing his tune about a self-imposed curfew. "We might as well do the night in."

"We've crossed that line," you tell him, as if he doesn't know.

"It's too late, this has been started."

This is drunk talk and you feel kinship that only people who look at bottles as though they are filled with whole lives do.

"What do you want to drink?" you ask, going inside to the pulsing music.

"I can't decide," he says loudly.

"Me, neither," you say, almost lying, knowing exactly what you want. Everything.

During rainstorms, back when Zachary was a skinny boy, the lame joke that went on around the playground went something like this: "You'd better hold onto a pole or you'll fly away." He never did fly away, and he didn't fully believe that it was possible. Still, sometimes if he stayed under the breezeway instead of going to the library during recess, he'd stand alone and when nobody was looking, he'd grab onto one of the metal poles just in case. He always wondered if any of them saw, if they knew they'd gotten the best of him. He pretended to be sick every day that it rained. And when he was forced to go, he'd usually escape to the library, where he'd challenge himself to read more books than anybody else in school. And there was no wind to blow him away.

Even the teachers were concerned. They called his mother, worried about his antisocial behavior, praising his academic performance, concerned about his pale emaciation. His mother assured them of what was true, which was that he ate all the time. "I can't help it," he remembered saying to one of the lunchroom ladies who always told him to eat everything on his plate. She weighed over two hundred pounds.

The doctors did all the tests, only to find no anemia, no nothing. The social workers came out once to check his mother's house. He was sure that they only did this to the people in his neighborhood, because of the way they talked to his mother like she was stupid. In the kitchen they found freezers and cabinets so full of food that the polyestered social workers must have felt ridiculous, but they never apologized. After they were gone, he saw the look of unwarranted shame on his mother's face.

As elementary school turned hauntingly into junior high, the doctors told him to eat bananas. He was sure by the way they all acted that he was bound to have a heart attack like his father, at any moment. The bananas didn't work and he was still a little afraid of strong winds. To him the wind was like the currents of water in the river by his house. They seemed all consuming, powerful to the point where they could send him in whatever direction they chose.

The first bottle of pills was not to kill himself. At fourteen, he ordered a bottle of amino acids and ate them all within three *days, never lifting a weight. Thinking that one day he'd magically wake up and be as big as the junior varsity football players. Or at least as strong as the basketball team.*

All of this made gym class a nightmare. He never dressed out, not wanting people to see his skinniness in the locker room. There were others who never dressed out either. That's where he smoked his first joint, with those guys in their Def Leppard T-shirts and Wrangler jeans. He liked this kind of flying away, because unlike the wind, he was in control of it. And he always landed safely.

Around this time, his sister, Candice, picked him up from school a few times after her shift as a nurse. She was much older and a little on the wild side. She'd take him riding around town, ELO and Rod Stewart cranked up full blast. He refused the first few times that she tried to give him coke, which she used a key to dig into the bag and snort. He was amazed that she could do this while driving somewhat sanely. He eventually gave in.

Later, he saw the bottles in her glove compartment. Things he knew that she'd taken from the hospital where she worked. And he knew that she couldn't be drinking it. That's when he went to stay with her in New Orleans. In her tiny hovel on St. Charles, not far from where Anne Rice created her vampires, he snored coke the first few nights. Then after seeing Candice and her cute boyfriend take turns coming in and out of the bathroom, he entered, slowly. That apartment was the quietest room he'd ever been in. All of them high, were afraid to make noise.

"Do you share needles?" he asked.

"Never."

"Will you hit me?"

She seemed shocked. "Are you sure?" Then, "All right, I'll give you a little."

He made a mark with his fingernail on the side of the new syringe so he'd know which one was his. And he just let her do it. It was nothing more than watching the syringe fill up the way he'd watch it when his mother took him to the hospital to find out why he was so thin. But this time, after Nurse Candice had drawn the blood, she pushed it all back into him. He stepped away and within moments, before he even had a chance to leave the bathroom and enter the living room, it hit him like an uncontrollable wind. On fire to the point of melting, he flew his way to a seated position on the floor. Candice's boyfriend was on the couch, and by just looking at him, Zachary felt like he did when he came after frantically jerking off to thoughts of him. This was sex and food all in one. When Candice returned from the bathroom, he said to her, "Now I understand why you do it."

"Shhh...now be quiet and enjoy it."

In the kitchen, the gorgeous boyfriend was burning tiny bits of paper on the stove, trying to set the apartment on fire. Just like Zachary had done when he was a kid. So he somehow talked him out of it. That's when they did some more, then went to buy more. After a week, he thought he saw his sister floating in the bathtub in a blood-soaked robe. Then he realized it was just the robe. But he knew he had to go, to leave before a robe like that became his teenage shroud. He left, not knowing that it was the beginning of a war.

Back home, he withdrew into his bedroom, crash-landing without his family even knowing. He couldn't tell his mother, because she would have had that look that she had when the social workers accused her of starving him to death. Even when he woke up screaming because of the snakes and children he saw falling from the ceiling, they didn't know. Not even when he sweated his clothes until he looked like a drowned rat did they know. He learned then that it sometimes took a junkie to know one. And each time someone in the house dropped a fountain pen or a pencil, he'd go running, thinking that it must be syringe waiting for him.

Three days later, he wished that he could go back to the place beneath the bleachers where he'd smoked pot with the grit boys. That all seemed so innocent compared to this. He was getting over this getting-over period and wanted to pretend it never happened. He blocked it out when he could and won-

dered how much skinnier it made him. When these days of sour Southern sweat wore off, he felt a little older physically, but younger mentally.

Then he started eating a lot again, and when it rained he loved to be in it. He loved the way the wind felt and held onto nothing, knowing that he was more powerful than the wind.

From then on, he tried to push the whole binge into that place where he kept his nightmares.

21

Wasted. A bar at closing time seems like a foreign land. But in New Orleans many of the bars never close. So the feeling of being in a city that makes its own rules has soaked you, so much so that you find it hard to rise to your feet. The fact that Zachary is with you helps. He is not as high as you, but still he is floating above the bench, too. Over the past few hours this bench has become yours and his. The sharp pocketknife in your back pocket makes you consider carving your initials into the wooden seat. But you are too far gone to do this accurately.

The sun, it is rising. The way it lights up the buildings in this city makes you imagine that you are in another country. You imagine it's what the buildings in places like Europe looked like before the bombs turned them into constructed skeletons. But you can't be sure, because you were never in those countries. In your war, the buildings were never glorious, only the land, and that was where the danger forced you to forget about any beauty that surrounded you.

The sun against these buildings blinds you. You flinch, knowing that bombs exploding always impair your vision. And like before, you wrap your arms around yourself, rocking in the light. Then you are reminded that you are not in this world alone.

Zachary reaches out to you. His hands, like bandages that you know only nurses usually have, cover your eyes. They are soft and long and press just gently enough to make the jumpy spots mixed with blackness go away. His hands are shaking a little when he takes them away, you can see. Vision reset.

You wonder what he thinks of you. This is not the first time he's seen you in this state. Maybe he thinks this is your constant way of being. It is. Constantly.

"I can drive you home," he tells you.

This is good to know. Otherwise you can see your-self spending days on the streets of New Orleans drunk, getting sucked off and looking for bombs to blow yourself up with.

"Drive me," you say. "Please."

He seems more powerful than you right now, unlike last night with his face shoved into a bag of powder. As you look at him watching the morning, he is as beautiful in this coked-out morning as he was in that wasted evening. He is all full of pale beauty that reads death, but makes you want to kiss him on his blood-red lips.

He tries to help you up, the shakes start, revealing a truth. The shakes are coming from him. He's weak, too. Standing is hard for him as well. He can't stand without wobbling and twitching to the point where you know that the only strength he has ever had has been left behind in some Mississippi field.

"Here," you say, handing him two Valium, which he obviously needs to calm down. The birds perch on the balcony ledge, making sounds that, if translated, would probably say something to the effect of "wake up." You'd be embarrassed by your own state if you weren't too far gone to care.

Then he hands you the coke. It's yet another bag. He holds the straw for you, just like last night. You are both trying to sober up, by continuing to mix Valiums and coke. Leveling off.

"We'll even out," he says, placing the blow into his pocket. "When we reach that balance, I'll drive us home."

You nod. "In that tank?" you ask, referring to your old truck and green vehicles you remember from years ago.

"What?" he asks, confused.

"Nothing."

As the birds begin to fly all around and the bar backs begin their morning sweep of the balcony, you two sit. "I can't believe that we ran into each other," you say, sobering up, or at least leveling off.

He stands up; the Valium must have kicked in because he's less shaky. On the balcony he joins the birds in their morning glory. You wonder what it would be like to see him jump, to see him fly from balcony to balcony with the birds.

"Do you want me to drive us back now?" He turns to you, asking this in a way that lets you know that if you say no, he would be okay with it.

"Please."

Now you are both able to stand and walk, hoping the mix stays with you long enough to get you home. Destinations. But he helps you with the walk inside the bar, through its emptiness. The only people inside are those whose lovers have left them cold with only a rough hangover to remember them by.

"Where are you parked?"

"Jax Brewery."

By this time, the streets are like those of the busiest city on earth. It is amazing to see people with their briefcases on their way to work. Initially you assume that everybody else spent the night like you.

As you two walk, your sides occasionally brush against each other. You wish you had stayed a little more sober last night. You are still staggering a bit and he has to catch you at one point as you near the parking lot.

"Let's walk past the water," he says. "Just for a moment. I don't come here often."

You agree verbally as your body screams no. At the Riverwalk, where the moon ruled the night, you lean as he stoops.

"Look," he says, rising with a red carnation—one of many which are still scattered and wind-blown from the night before. "This is for you," he says.

You take it, wanting to lean against a wall of steel. The red, the smell of flowers like a funeral, overwhelms you. You reach for a wooden pole, but misstep and fall back like a bad dancer on a stage. The ground hurts.

You feel him raise you, holding you up, the carnation stuck in your shirt pocket like a fat, spreading blood stain. To be led home, to lean on.

"Thank you," you say with a swallow, leaning all the way into him, awaiting the field in Mississippi.

Opera.

22

When you open your eyes you are back in Petulia. Collapsing has the power of a time machine. Blacking out can transport you from a forest of bourbonesque cement to a grassy land empty of all but yesterday. At least this time you had Zachary to help you get home.

You sit in the truck briefly after it is parked in front of the trailer. Zachary finally gets out. Three p.m. never felt so much like early morning. "Wanna come in for a drink?"

He shakes his blond head. "Nah, I gotta work at five."

"How can you manage that?"

"Got something to keep me going."

He looks into your eyes as though you are a full-length mirror. "Recognize yourself?" he finally asks, knowing that you can see your reflection in each other's eyes.

As you stand in front of the truck, you get a good look at him. You want to touch his T-shirt and to kiss his lips, which are even redder now.

"Now that was a night out," he says.

"It was."

Standing in front of the truck, neither one of you says much. He takes out a handkerchief and blows his nose. You need to blow yours, too, but don't want him to see you. There is a little blood when he blows, but you both pretend that you don't notice it. It matches his lips. "Are you sure you don't want a drink?"

"I want one, but I've got to go to work."

You nod, truly understanding, truly wanting one yourself.

"I guess I could have a quick one," he finally says.

"Come on in."

You lead him through the screen door, hoping the place isn't too much of a mess. Except for the scattered clothes, it's clean. Besides, since Gina took most of the stuff, there's nothing to clutter it.

In the kitchen, you have him sit down as you pour two vodkas with lemon twists. You don't want him to leave. Loneliness.

"Where's your wife?"

"I don't have one."

"You used to."

"How do you know?" You're both sitting at the table now.

"I saw you with her before in town. Once you came into where I work. She ordered a lot of iced tea."

"Well, she left me."

"Too bad."

He's drinking fast. Maybe he'll have time for two. "Yeah, too bad."

"Kids?"

"One, she lives in the city."

"Cool."

"So you live here all alone."

Now that he's mentioned it, you have to admit it. "Yeah, I guess I do."

"How long?"

"A day."

He gags a little on the rest of his drink, and you pour him his second one. These things come in threes. He'll get there. "What was your wife like?"

"Betty Crocker."

He laughs. "Worse things. Worse people to marry, I'm sure."

"Is all of this what led you to the bars?" He looks around. "One of these nights, you'll pass out for good."

"Yeah, imagine dying in a booth at a hick gay bar."

"It rivals that guy's jumping."

He is right. You pour yourself another drink, surprised he's already set for a third.

"Remember the first time we met, when you bought me back to your place?" you ask. "I loved that morning."

"Really?"

"I wanted to touch your shirt all day after that."

"Like now?"

"Like now."

You reach out your left hand, your right one firmly gripping your drink. And you trace his skin and bones through his shirt.

"Too skinny, huh?"

You shake your head. "No." And to prove it, you touch him again. It's like touching another person for the first time. Each bone in his chest holds its own story. You want to read them all.

"What about you? Where's your family?"

"My dad is dead. Has been for years. My mom lives around here. She runs the fabric store. I moved out of my apartment and back in with her. I only admit that because I'm so high." His face is a pink that verges on red. "We haven't heard from my sister in over a year. She's probably either dead in some motel room with a needle in her arm, or in jail." He takes a big drink of the vodka. "And my brother, well, he's dead, too. Leukemia, he was only twenty-six."

"How old are you?"

"That's how old I am now. That's why it feels old to me." He sets his glass down and takes out the coke, doing a couple of lines, offering some to you, which of course you inhale, like it's the last time you'll ever do anything to get high.

He reaches out and touches your face. Slowly. "You are a good-looking man," he says. "Your wife sure lost out." He traces your face the way you traced his chest. You wonder if he sees the stories in the lines of your face.

Then you take both of your hands and place them on his face and for one brief moment you kiss his vibrant red lips. Hunger. He blinks slowly and settles back in his chair. "Do you kiss a lot of men?" you ask.

"No," he says. "They don't kiss me. You know what they want. I lived in New York for a while. I'm not built enough. They want a poster, I can never be a poster." You rub his left cheek. "What did you do before you got married?"

"Oh, stuff. I'll rent you a movie. I don't like to talk about it much."

"That's cool," he says, checking the clock. It's four now. "Let's do this. Tell me the worst mistake you ever made."

"Huh?"

"It's fair, and fun. But only if you want to."

"No."

"Come on."

You don't like this pressure, so you get up and get some more ice, then begin to walk back and forth across the kitchen. The images aren't melting away anymore. They're returning and filling your eyes. Even this boy that you're so taken with becomes part of it. "You are like them," you say angrily. "I can see you. Death settling in with a tube down your throat. Bombs blasting. Bullets in backs. Firing until you kill everyone within sight. Is that the mistake you're looking for?"

"I'm sorry, man. I didn't know."

"Now you do. I'm one of them." You are drunk now and it's showing, you feel yourself growing louder, wondering why you invited him in.

"I gotta go," he says. "I'll be late for work."

"No. You tell me now. Your big mistake."

"It doesn't matter."

"Tell me. It's the only way the game can end fairly."

He seems shaken, so you put your hand into his and hold firmly. "Starting this game was a bad idea," he sighs.

He can't speak. You squeeze his shoulder. "Fairness," you say again.

"I opened the back door," he suddenly tells you.

"For what?"

"I opened the back door."

The bottle gets emptier, five o'clock passes.

Mistakes.

Zachary was five, or at least he was comfortable believing this was his age when he opened the door. Everyone was sleeping in the big white house next to the church. He shared a room with his sister and when he was young, he didn't mind such things as not having his own space. But somehow, during the night, the insomnia he always experienced took over. And he wandered from the bedroom, like he actually had somewhere to go. The hallway was long, and he paused beneath the attic fan before entering the kitchen. He stood there, a boy full of ideas and wonders.

In the spring, in houses like this, the screen door to the back of the house was always latched, but the air from it was pulled in by the attic fan. While he knew that Uncle Roy was somebody he'd been told to stay away from, he still walked to the back door and lifted the latch. Then Uncle Roy was inside.

But Zachary ran away, to the other end of the hallway, knowing that he'd eventually go back into the kitchen, just to see what Uncle Roy was doing.

He paused for a long moment, this time beneath the attic fan, then walked into a kitchen that was no longer his or his mother's and father's; it belonged to Uncle Roy. There were two bottles beneath the table. Once contained orange juice and the other one was full of a clear liquid.

Maybe he had gone back into the kitchen because Uncle Roy drew great Popeye cartoons and had won first place in the "battle of the bands" at the county fair. Maybe it was because when Zachary had torn the head from his sister's baby doll on Christmas Day, Uncle Roy had laughed and said, "Oh, son," like maybe it wasn't completely bad.

He swallowed hard; the saliva from that moment would

stay with him for years after. The hands, they smelled like the smaller streets of New Orleans, where his father had once taken him for a haircut. His breath was like orange juice. Zachary wanted his mother to serve orange juice for breakfast in the morning. He heard a noise and could have sworn that the refrigerator door had opened and closed by itself. He wondered if he could fit on one of the shelves, to escape this citric moment.

The cabinets in the kitchen were low, blue, and peeling, and his head went down low and back, his scalp scraping splinters along the way.

He didn't see Uncle Roy now. This was because his head was turned sharply to the right, and he wondered if it could snap. Now he knew why they had told him to stay away from Uncle Roy, but he couldn't figure out why the kitchen table was spinning like a top on the floor. He watched the table spin out of control as the noise from the attic fan reminded him of a freight train.

When the window opened and closed all by itself, he didn't even question why. It was as though this is what all windows did at times like this. He almost felt that he was making it all happen by looking at these things.

Then his head was farther back, but straighter. And he saw the single lightbulb hanging there above the sink. He was sure his skull would be rolling around and spinning with the table, hoping it would lift from the ground and take either him or Uncle Roy with it.

His back was hurting, the lightbulb went off, then on again. But it wasn't scary like a haunted house. Instead, it was a great distraction from the pain down there. Then the light went out again, and this time it did not come back on.

Later, there was a little light in the bedroom when his mother told him that everything was okay. Even though he heard his other uncle, the shell-shocked Uncle Danny who lived with them, yelling at Uncle Roy near the front door, he was told that everything was all right. He wondered what his father would have done if he had not been working on the *shrimp boats offshore.*

At dawn, after he was awakened by Aunt Eartha's roosters, Zachary saw something else move. He saw a tiny train with all of the letters of the alphabet using the headboard of his bed for tracks. And it went back and forth. This scared him more than anything the night before. He found the only way to stop it was to take his pillow and hold it until he fell asleep.

The next day, as he watched **Sesame Street***, shell-shocked Uncle Danny brought him some Fruit Loops. He watched the Muppets, realizing how easily they could fall apart, how their heads could just snap back and off. He knew that while Uncle Danny was fixing his cereal, he could crawl into the television and join the Muppets, because last night he had learned that he was one.*

A few minutes later, he sat there, glad that he hadn't started school yet, eating cereal, and watching Big Bird be really nice and tall. And every once in a while he'd look over at Uncle Danny, who had come into the kitchen just as Uncle Roy was finishing the violence with his penis. Uncle Danny was scrubbing the front door, trying to wash the blood away from where he'd nearly beaten Uncle Roy to death the night before.

23

After he is gone, stumbling from the house in a drunken state on his way, late for work, it still seems like he is inside the trailer. You look around to make sure that he didn't forget anything, and except for a straw caked with powder on the inside, there is nothing that he's left. You wonder how he'll work or if he'll even work. You wanted him to stay with you and talk about things that wouldn't have any significance to anyone who wasn't in your states of mind. The talking you did with Zachary could have gone on until the entire roof of the trailer caved in. And you could have touched him some more, while all along waiting patiently for him to touch you. But now that he is gone, there is nothing to do but recline on the slanting, afghaned couch, channel-flipping, knowing that you can't lie on this couch forever. At least not until a dream comes. The phone rings. Life.

"Gina?"

"Gary, is it true?" Gina sounds concerned at first, and when you don't answer immediately she gets angry. "Is it true?" she asks, yelling.

You sigh and lie back down, wanting to hang up, never wanting her to call unless she has something smoother to say.

"Probably. Whatever it is, it's probably true."

"Is Lula..." She stops for a moment and takes a deep breath. There is nothing that annoys you more than phone breathing.

"Well," she starts. Then she says it all at once, "Is it true that she's working in a gay bar in the city? Is it? Miss Ima Jean's son, you know, the funny one, said he saw here there, mixing drinks, dancing around with those people." Gina isn't crying, but there is panic in her voice.

"It's true."

You are amazed at the way Gina's voice has changed since she left the house. It's like her voice has grown deeper. As if she is talking through a walkie-talkie. She's rougher now. Maybe you sound the same way when you leave the house. But you're not used to hearing her sound like this, and as usual you don't say much. You wait for her to signal in from the wooded house she is sharing with the cop. Then you remember it's a modern telephone.

"What are we gonna do with her?" she asks, sounding angry again.

"Nothing."

"Nothing? Oh, come on, Gary. We can't..."

"I'll talk to her."

"Sober?"

"Sober." You don't tell this wife of yours that you are sleeping off a ton of chemicals and that you've already talked to Lula.

"So, Gary, how are you?" She seems to really want to know and this surprises you.

"Good."

"Lonely?" She asks this in a slow, confused way, like she's actually asking herself the question.

"Not much. How's life on the other side of town?"

"Lovely. You should see the house."

You rub against the ancient afghan, then sit up, reaching for a Valium. Repossession. "Lula's a grown woman."

"But you will talk to her."

"Yes." You are lying, and you know it, and it doesn't matter.

"I can't believe we turned out such a child."

You throw your head back. It is getting dark outside, like one of those nights where cars find their way to the edge of curvy roads and burst into flames.

"I should go," she adds. "Bowling night."

"Have fun." Before anybody hangs up, you stop her.

"Gina, I think that Lula is fine. She's happy, and she looks good."

"What? You saw her!"

"I talked to her."

"You what? Couldn't you have called me and told me?"

"She's good, Gina. Leave her alone."

You hear her smack her lips. "All right...all right... But what do I tell people?"

"What people?"

"Any of them."

"Tell them whatever you want."

"You sound tired." Her voice sounds less radio-active now. Meltdown.

"I am. Call me later." She sounds more stable. You've never heard her go in so many different directions with her emotions in such a short period of time.

You're sure she's clipping her nails or putting on makeup as she discusses this. She's paying attention, but mostly to her own words. Sermons. You hang up without saying goodbye and lie on the afghan, thinking of how she shouldn't even bother calling. It cuts both ways. To stab and to be stabbed. Sensitive backs.

On the couch, you think of Zachary's long fingers unlatching the door and walking to you.

You wonder if Lula will like him. It's a bit early to worry about these things, but still you wonder about it as you fall asleep. In your dream, he is a poster, all beautiful and thin. Arms and legs never seemed so long. His fingers go on for miles. It's as if he could cover the entire state of Texas with his limbs. And in this dream, Zachary steps out of the poster and jumps into a pool somewhere in a place far away. Then there is light.

You open your eyes. At the screen window, you see flashlights. You wonder how long they've been watching. So you sit up. "Gooks!" you scream, tearing off through the house, finally hiding in a closet in the hall. When the fear has lifted a little, you creep from the closet holding a gun that is just in your imagination. You turn the corner to find that the light is moving away. Closer to the window, you see a couple of figures moving away. Then you hear a car door.

You close the window. Night watch haunts you even though you've seen worse. Tonight you refuse to hear the guns and the brief rustling of the trees.

So you lie there, now beneath the afghan, wondering why the lights came so close to you as you slept. And you try and think of good things. Like how you have almost a whole bottle of Valium left. And how Zachary could reappear just in time.

In your attempt to sleep, you hear cars passing slowly on the street. Knowing that beautiful boys like Zachary never return to houses like yours. Even the field seems like a foreign land now. So when the opera music begins, you sleep, knowing that it will last until you get up and leave at 6 a.m. Work.

24

You don't sleep all the way through. At 3 a.m. you awake, completely disoriented and exhausted in that middle-of-the-night sort of way. You raise the window to get some air and to hear the opera. You're a little angry that he didn't come to your place just to let you know he was around. Tossing, you knock over a glass of water and leave it on the stained carpet. Then you rise, no longer afraid of the flashlights that blinded you hours ago and drove you to the closet. Across the way, you see your boy and his radio beside him.

The sky begins to lighten, if only a little. Enough for you to see Zachary sitting beside his radio. You close your eyes. Growing old, you've missed your chance at a love like Zachary. In your vibrant youth, maybe you could've been his lover. But you are no longer youthful and perhaps not even sane. Feeling old never hurt so bad.

You fix yourself a vodka on the rocks. And it tastes splendid. Then you carry it to the only place you know where you feel you belong, to sit. The front steps.

You're wearing your leftovers from the night before, but only you know this and don't especially care. Vodka makes you feel this way. Apathetically aware. It takes a while for you to realize that the music has stopped.

Zachary is staring at the ancient scarecrow. The music stays dead, the other man not moving. That's when you stand up and move closer to the highway. A cop car passes. It seems as though that's all that there are around this town. When you reach the field, Zachary turns to you. "This thing survives forever," he says.

You feel ridiculous for having been jealous of a scarecrow. "Sometimes I think it is a real person," you say.

He laughs. "It is. It's you." He pulls you close and

makes you face it.

"It looks like you," you point out to him.

"I think it looks like you," he jokes back.

"It has held up well," you say, almost frightened by seeing you and Zachary all combined in one stickly creation. "What happened to the music?"

He walks over to the box and puts on something you've never heard, but want to. "I thought you'd stop by after work since you were out here."

"Nah, I figured I'd make you arrive instead of visiting you."

You move closer to him and he walks toward you, kicking at the toes of your sneakers. Then he stands on top of them. He is beyond a pin-up now. He is all flesh and bone, his eyes magnets, his lips beyond porn. But you don't kiss him. Instead you pull him close, and he dances on your feet. The two of you move in slow circles around the scarecrow as if it too is part of the dance. Ménage-à-trois.

Your face against his, he whispers, "After my story earlier, you're afraid to touch me too much," he says.

"This is enough for me."

He laughs and squeezes your arm. "Hey, who really is the scarecrow around here?"

You move a little closer before his red lips hit yours, and you hope that yours turn the same color. And you hold each other, ignoring the traffic on the highway, moving in a way that goes beyond dancing as you or most people have ever known it.

The three of you in the field, waiting for the sun to fully rise. You briefly think about work, but things like work are passing thoughts. You lick your lips and taste the redness, all the while dancing. You are sure that even when the music stops, the dancing will continue.

To be in someone's arms, on green grass, makes the trailer seem as though it doesn't even exist. A secure new world with an old name called home.

25

The birds come to the window long after the alarm clock has rung. You heard them in your sunrise sleep, but like the alarm clock, let them pass you by. The phone keeps ringing, and you don't answer it. Yet you still don't want to let the work you care little about pass you by. It's because, besides your trailer, your job is the only sturdy thing that you have. Your back hurts in a way that is always brought on by cheap couches. You remember the night before in bits and pieces. A dream that was real. Strange lights at your window, blinding you like a flashback, but the heat from them let you know that it was all too real. Maybe it was Zachary. Maybe it was nothing more than a car turning around in the driveway seeming as though it was just at the window. You wonder if your eyes are damaged from the brightness, because it seems to take longer for them to adjust to the room, which is darker than usual. But you know that a boy dancing on your feet, guiding you in circles, across the grass of the night, was no dream. You know this because your boots beneath the coffee table come into focus and you see the prints of his sneakers on the top of each of them. They are perfectly matched, as though he didn't even take a wrong step. Not in a long time have you danced without the fear of falling, able to, even as someone else shared your boots. Who was holding who?

When you look out the window, it is clear why the light is like this. Outside the newborn day has arrived with defects in it. It is all bruised gray and black with only slight lines of white forcing their way through. It is all mismatched pieces of a Monday sky before a storm. It's another sky from the one you crept beneath last night. This sky is like a flawed infant, as if it has been sprayed with something to make it monstrous. Napalm.

When the phone rings this time, you answer it. It's Richard. "Rainy one," he says.

"Yep," you agree. Though you need the money, you want the day off anyway.

"Say, we're in a flash-flood watch," he tells you. You can hear his television in the background and the weather man talking.

"I'm going back to bed," you tell him.

"If it clears up later, I'll call you. That house needs to be built by the end of next month."

"Yeah, okay." You hang up, knowing that he will go on forever about how the new workers have thrown work all off schedule. Also knowing that it's not going to clear up. Richard always says that, even during hurricanes.

You yawn your way toward the bathroom, then you hear the knock. A pounding at the door. You forget about peeing and go to open the door. "Daddy," Lula cries, throwing her arms around you, almost pulling you down the steps. You almost don't recognize her with her shiny hair and makeup. Only the way she holds onto your elbow lets you know that she is not an imposter. "My friend Organic came with me. I was wondering if I could get my dresser. He has a truck."

You see the pickup, a figure in the passenger's seat. "Sure, come on in."

She motions to him and follows you inside. "You sure it's okay to drive back in the weather?" you ask.

Her friend enters, looking like he was born in 1969 and is still dressing like it. Tie-dye. "This is Organic. Organic, this is my dad." You shake hands, wondering if he is one of you or an actual boyfriend of hers. One thing that you do notice is how his glasses almost perfectly match hers. You are happy when he takes her hand.

"Where's Mama?" she asks.

"You guys want some coffee?" you ask, instead of answering her.

"No, thanks." Organic sits down on the couch and stares blankly across the room, looking more relaxed than stoned. His hair is longer than hers. He is thin. They fit.

"None for me, Daddy," she says sitting down beside Organic. Young. Love. "Where's Mama?" she asks again.

"She's not here." You now realize that you never told her that Gina has left. You wish that Gina had done this.

"Yeah, so..."

"So, what?" You pull up a kitchen chair, still needing to pee, but feeling trapped, like you're at a dinner party of tough questions that you can't break away from.

"So where is she?"

"She left."

"Where to?"

"She left."

"I know. You just said that. Where? To the store? To the beauty parlor?"

"She left me," you manage to say, craving a Valium. This what they are prescribed for. Still, you can't take one in front of them.

Lula doesn't move. Not even a muscle in her face makes any sort of statement. Then she nods. "Wow. Where's she living?"

"Call her, she'll tell you." You go to the refrigerator and take a pen and paper from the magnetic notepad. His number is there in Gina's handwriting. She left it behind so you'd know how to get in touch with her, but you don't intend to use it. You hand it to Lula. "She left this for you," you say, handing it to her.

"Wow," she repeats, looking around the room. "I guess a lot of stuff is gone. It's so funny, Daddy. I was so looking forward to seeing you that I wasn't even worried about the things in the house." She stands up and begins to wander around the living room, her eyes finding the places of where things used to be. "She took a lot."

"Only the good stuff," you laugh.

"I'm gonna have some orange juice," you say as an excuse. "Organic, what do you say?"

"None for me," Lula says still checking out the blank spaces around the room.

"I'll have some anyway," he says blankly.

In the kitchen, you fumble with the bottle of Valium and take two of the blues, washing them down with the orange juice. When you walk back into the room, Organic takes the glass from you. He, too, is walking around, gazing at the place as though he's been here before. As though he can see what Gina took. "What used to be here?" he asks, his love beads dangling from his neck. You don't know what empty space he's talking about, there are so many. "A calendar," you say, thinking he's talking about the space on the wall above the cedar chest. You're also reminded of the year it is not.

"No, here," he says, pointing directly at the chest.

"An aquarium," you say, wondering why he cares.

"She took the aquarium!" Lula gasps. "Oh, Daddy."

"She said she wasn't going to take it, but in the end she decided to." You sit back down. From the window you can see the sky is not quite as dark. The scarecrow is over there, watching intensely. You are sure it can see straight through the window and walls of the trailer, filling itself up with this moment, which is alternating between mundane and intense. "You look great, Lula. The city is treating you good, huh?"

"I guess. Organic seems to think so."

"Yep," he says, wandering around, like he's lost in a room a hundred times this size.

"She'll come back," she repeats.

"No, Lula." You take her hand. "She will not."

And you can tell by the way that she holds onto you that she finally believes you. "You mean I left, then she left, and you're the only one not gone. It's not right, Daddy." She begins to cry. "It's not."

Organic finds his way to her and puts his hand on her shoulder. She stands up and loses her face in his neck.

"Lula. It is right. Believe me, it is the right thing." You are trying to convince yourself of everything you say to her, knowing it all to be true. "It's a new life for all of us. It's right. It's a good thing. I've never lied to you, Lula. And I'm not going to say that sometimes it's not too quiet, but it always was after you left. But I kind of like it."

"Are you happy?"

"Yes." Half-truths. She almost smiles as she wipes away her tears. "Now how about us getting that dresser in the van before it rains."

"Yep." Organic has said this favorite word again.

"All right," Lula agrees.

The dresser is not so heavy, but you wish that Lula was helping instead of Organic. His small frame isn't made for this.

"This used to be my place," she says with pride.

"Really?" he grunts as he follows you with the light end through the door of the bedroom.

As you go down the steps you realize that it's not looking so rainy anymore. The light is a little stunning to you, causing you to almost drop the dresser. Once you dropped a dead man, and you never went back to pick him up. Then you began to drop them all of the time because that's what you did when people became heavy. And now Gina has done it to you.

"Oh, fuck!" Organic says as his end slips out of his hand and slides swiftly to the grass. "Sorry," he says, before picking up the undamaged dresser again.

Lula opens the back door to the van where you slide the dresser in. The van is sparsely decorated and reeks of incense.

"The weather's looking better," Lula says.

"Yeah," you agree. "Why don't you two let me fix

you some breakfast?"

"We can't, Daddy. Organic's gotta be at work by noon."

"Yep," you find yourself saying. "All right. Organic, what do you do?"

"I'm a web-page designer." You know so little about this whole field that you decide he'd better explain it to you when you're plastered. Lula walks over and hugs you. "I'm sorry."

"For what? Next time, plan a longer visit. We'll plan something. Maybe we can barbecue."

"You look a lot better, Daddy. You don't look wasted."

Not yet, you think.

"We better get going," she says as Organic shakes your hand.

"You kids be careful," you say.

You wave to them as they pull away, wondering how many vans like that, with people like Organic, still roam the land. As you hit the steps and go back inside, you feel the pills beginning to work, glad Lula didn't stick around to witness the glaze you see in your eyes when you look in the bathroom mirror. Isolation.

Just before you've finished peeing, you hear the phone, but it stops after about five rings. In the living room, you see that Organic has left his nonorganic orange juice sitting on the cedar chest untouched. You take it and drink it in one greedy gulp, wondering if he dropped a goldfish or anything else into the glass. It burns going down. Your stomach feels like that a lot lately. Like a million fish swimming around inside of it.

The phone. Again. You answer it this time. It's Richard. "Looks like it's clearing up out there. Think we can get some work done."

"Yeah," you say, swearing it'll be the last time you ever answer the phone. "I'll be there in an hour."

From what you can see the sky has lightened to the point of brightness. Richard was right.

26

Refill day comes. Your countdown to the red-capsuled, blue-tabled day is here. These days when you get your freshly full bottle of pills have become a marker of your life.

You are Friday tired. It is that feeling that sets in each week at this time.

The traffic isn't helping as cars zig-zag in and out of lanes, turning the small town of Petulia into as much of a metropolis as it will ever be. The strip malls are packed. It is as though these people have never been to any store before. All this leads to an insanity of cars fighting their way down Main Street. A street only called that, you figure, because every city must have one.

But soon you turn left, channel-flipping, not listening to anything until George Strait hits the right spot, giving you a reason to settle back and enjoy the ride to the pharmacy. You're using the pharmacy just outside of Hattiesburg because they never give you a hard time. You've been going to more than one doctor, getting the same medications, hoping you can stay one step ahead of whoever it is that's supposed to keep track of such things.

Your arm is hanging out of the window, bent, with your hand tapping the door to "Amarillo by Morning." You body is unusually worn, even for a Friday. It was a rough week at work with Richard pushing you to get that house built. And it wasn't even much of a house in the end. Just a basic three-bedroom, wooden place for somebody to make their own. You are sure that whoever would buy a house like that will paint it yellow and plant tulips in the front yard.

This back road is treacherous and begins to curve, with you realizing how easy it would be to fly off the road and into a tree. Four of your friends did that when you were all in high school. None of them lived. Necks crack, bones break. It is also like the officer in Vietnam who kept promising you that he was going to crash his Jeep. And after he told you for the fifth time, he did it. You didn't believe him, the same way that you didn't believe your friends from the sixties would find themselves dying against a tall healthy pine tree.

George Strait songs always end too soon. You channel-flip, careful at each turn in the road. Side roads like this have no shoulder, so even when you feel your heart beating faster than it should, you can't pull over.

Aside from the deadly curves, it is nice out there. There are countless trees until you come to Murphy's farm. There, since your breathing has turned to hyperventilation, you pull over into the first driveway that you come to.

It is getting darker. You need to get to the pharmacy, but are too paralyzed to drive. Curves can do that to you.

You look all around the farm, able to picture Lula and Organic living in a place like this. You imagine them growing pot and her staying high on fiction. But then maybe you're thinking about the old Lula. The new one may have grown smaller in size but bigger in the way she views the world. When they visited earlier in the week, you really liked Organic. You liked the way he rushed to Lula's side even before she began to cry. And the way that when he dropped the dresser, he gasped as though it was a child.

The curves. You hate yourself for taking this road. The traffic would have pushed you into this frenzy, but the curves have pushed you in that same direction. The farm is quiet, except for the crickets. You seem to be the only person around for miles. This illegal parking spot is your world. You feel safe. Then you see it. The skull.

It is your skull on the hood of the truck, a little bloody. You blink, hoping it will go away, knowing it's for real only because you created it.

But it won't disappear. You wanted to be blinded now, like you were by the sun on a French Quarter balcony. Gunshots. You feel the car shake. "Down," you say again, throwing yourself across the seat which is your jungle of ripped vinyl seats and cheap tree-shaped air-freshener. You reach up, and pulling, bring down the entire rearview mirror, tossing it out of the window as far as you can throw. Grenades.

You rise slowly from the trees, which are nothing more than the thickest air you've ever felt in a vehicle. You hear them coming, the Viet Cong are on their way. Marching invisibly toward the car.

You freeze, staring ahead at the skull which is no longer yours. Instead, it has begun to transform itself into every person you ever saw bleeding from the face. They alternate in a way which you think is chrono-logical. You hope it is, anyway. At least that way, it will end sooner or later.

On the hood, the skull is now that of the tough officer who rammed his Jeep, resulting in his decap-itation. His image stays a while longer than the others. And you can hear him. "I'm tired of this motherfucking shit...I'm tired of this...I'm tired..."

You wonder if the blood of this conscious nightmare is staining the hood permanently. You are frozen, think-ing at first that you may be dead. Maybe you missed a curve and didn't even notice the crash. Then the faces begin to go backward, then forward, then become a bloody face that you don't ever remember seeing red. This is when you know you are not the dead one. It is the heads of their lives passing before you.

"They are dead," you say, pounding at the steering wheel, your left hand a little sore. "You are dead," you say again to the recurring images. Full circle. And then they are all gone, leaving you with nothing except a wet sweat, skipped heartbeats, and no rearview mirror.

You're surprised at how you control the moment. Other times you would have run across the earth, believing that eventually you would either time-travel back to Southeast Asia for a permanent vacation or be gunned down by men you knew as your enemies.

You crank the car back up. The road feels like your own again. All of the bad curves are out of your way. You want to know why you have grown less active in your fistfight with yourself. You think it should have been worse with Gina gone because you still miss her. And then there's Zachary, whom you haven't heard from in days.

For a couple of nights you stayed awake, hoping to hear his music in the field, but finally you gave up and took a Seconal instead. It helped you sleep through the grief of his not arriving.

It is strange that the two of you never exchanged phone numbers. You can't imagine him even having a home. Though you wonder if he still does.

It is getting late as you press your way to the small drugstore. The man is putting the closed sign on the door as you walk up to it. He shakes his head at first, but you stare at the sign calmly like it is a common sight. Like a bloody head on a truck's hood, he opens up.

"Come on in, Gary. I tell you, you're always late." He's already taken off his white coat and is wearing a pink polo shirt with some expensive jeans.

"Traffic," you excuse yourself.

"I'm glad to get your business. But do you have to come so far for your prescriptions?"

"No," you say bluntly, throwing your nearly maxed-out Visa card at him. You can't use your V.A. insurance here. The double prescriptions would show up on the computer.

He whistles as he fills your prescriptions. You feel that unique tinge of excitement as you hear him scraping the pills from the tray into the bottles. You browse around, wanting to buy everything you never needed. You don't even like shopping, but drugstores do this to you.

After you've paid and he's given you what you need, you feel like he's looking at you suspiciously. "You take too many pills," he says.

"That's my doctor's business and mine."

"Junkie," you hear him say under his breath as he lets you out the door and locks it behind you.

You want to bash the glass door open. You refrain by biting down on your bottom lip so hard that the sharpness of your teeth makes blood seep out.

You turn around so he can see what it is like to watch a man leaking blood. You want him to see red on a man's face just once. But too soon, he is in the back of the store paying no attention to you or the blood that is dripping down your chin.

Junkie.

You slow-ride away to Jethro Tull, completely in control, taking only one Valium. You contemplate going out to New Orleans but the Friday tiredness wins out. So you drive home, with no rearview mirror to catch a glimpse of your blood-stained lips. You lick at the blood, and it tastes like what you remember blood is supposed to taste like.

All the way back home, you feel alone, missing everyone you've ever known. Almost wishing you could hallucinate the skulls again just to keep you company. This time you wouldn't fear them, so naturally they don't come.

Even seeing your own head on the truck would have been a relief. Being with what you used to be always feels better than being alone.

But right now there is only you to take the curves sharply, wondering if any of the trees are calling out to you, with your name already chiseled in the wood.

27

A letter from Zachary arrives the same day Gina calls to talk about the legalities of divorce. In your mind, the divorce has already taken place. There is a gentleness to her voice, though. The anger that you saw welling up inside of her seems more controlled now. Maybe Eddie is the best thing that's happened to her. You still hate this thought. Jealousy is your weakness, and you know it.

Then Lula calls. She is even more pleasant. This is all happening on yet another tired Friday in what seems like a month of them. You put the letter on the coffee table and think about its contents as much as you think about your phone conversations.

"I love him, Daddy." Lula is ecstatic. "We're getting married. Do you approve?"

"Yes."

"Will you come to the wedding? It's just gonna be a small thing with some of our friends here in the French Quarter. And Daddy, I know you're shy, but you're so normal compared to a lot of Organic's friends. They're real freaks. You've got nothing to worry about. Just come."

"I'll be there..."

This is a contrast to the conversation with Gina, who is all business in a pleasant tone. "Six months before we can actually get a divorce," she says, pausing for the longest time.

"Fine."

"I guess it'll have to be." She stops again. This is the most real silence you've ever had in a phone conversation. "Gary," she finally says in a way that you know is sincere. "How are you?"

"I'm good."

"Lula says you look more handsome than ever."

"I am," you tease.

"Oh, Gary, we did have some fun early on. Even later. We did have some fun."

You fumble with the letter on the table. The wind is blowing in, and you weigh it down with the current issue of *TV Guide*.

"Gary?"

"Yes...yes...we did have fun."

Her laugh gradually ceases. "Gary, one thing. I know you've been sleeping on the couch lately. Now don't think I'm being greedy, but...well...do you think I could have our bed? I've got this nice one here. And you can have it. It's just that this is a nice house, and it just doesn't match. And you know how bad my back is. I need the mattress. Like I said, you can have this one..."

"Come and get it," you tell her.

"Really?" Overjoyed.

"Sure. I can't stand the sight of it. In fact I was going to throw it out," you lie, not caring that she probably knows that you are. "In fact, if you don't come get it today, I'll get rid of it."

You wonder if part of it is that you just want to see her, see someone. "But I don't want the one you have."

"Are you sure?"

"I'm sure."

"I'll be there. Are you sure you're okay?" she asks. Of course, she probably expected the fight you didn't give her.

"I am fine."

All you can do is drink after a call like that. Straight bourbon and a little Seconal in a spoon, mixed with sugar to cover the bitterness. It still tastes disgusting but does the trick.

Maybe if she takes the bed, you can finally sleep in that room again. A sleeping bag on the floor seems a comfortable idea now. Camping out in the safety of your own tent of a trailer is a beautiful thought.

In the bedroom, where you hardly ever venture, you look at yourself in the mirror. Maybe you do look a little better. Even fucked up, you don't hate you as much. You only wish, like everyone else, that you were younger. You even like the way your tan looks against your white underwear. You want somebody else to see what you see for this quick moment, and love it.

You begin to take the bed apart. It's almost fun. Destruction. You wish you had an ax. Instead you take it apart civilly so she can get it and go. You catch a glimpse of the scarecrow across the way and wonder if he approves of your handing the bed over with such ease.

You hear a car door slam, then another. Eddie must be with her. That's when you rush into your jeans and flannel shirt, take the letter from the coffee table, and exit through the back door.

You walk across the highway and sit by the scarecrow. You watch as Gina and the cop she loves carry their new old bed away piece by piece.

Then you turn away from them. "Can you believe this?" you ask the scarecrow, wondering what he would say if he were an answerer. Finally you open the letter, still recovering from what has happened in your life over the past few weeks. You hear Gina call your name, but ignore her.

You open Zachary's letter with warranted fear and apprehension:

Dear Gary,

I am here in this room in my mother's house where I have been for the past three weeks listening to music in the dark. Afraid to leave the room, because each time I do, I get into trouble. There are so many ways. And yet only a few of my mistakes come to mind. The white dust, the big cities with men who love me the wrong way with their hands. I crashed here, unable to move. *I finally began to eat, to disappear so I can go out again and be myself. I never have been. The wind, the people in town, even when I am in cities far away, push me. I always say yes and want to say no five minutes later. No matter what the situation is, I am always at a loss.*

The field was the only place where I could go, but one night a few weeks ago the cops came and took me in for disturbing the peace. Not because anyone complained, but because I am not like them and can't lie about it. When they ask me. So now I am on probation because I listened to music on the land they consider theirs.

I hate the darkness of this room. I hate being back here.

But have been through this many times before, wherever I've been. Paris, New York, Los Angeles. I've always found myself stuck in a room. I create my own prisons.

In the past I've always gotten out. There is always a darkened room somewhere waiting.

Like I said already, every time I say yes, I mean no right after. I think of everything when I think about you and hold myself in the night.

Five minutes pass and pass again and still I say yes.

> *Best,*
> *Zachary*

You close the letter and put your hand over your mouth, feeling the lips he talked about, feeling the whiskers he touched.

You lie there, wasted, staring up at the scarecrow Zachary built, wanting it to tell you where he is. You hear Gina and her man pull away.

Lying still on the grass, you hear the music and sit up to look for him. But like skulls on hoods and Vietnamese soldiers in the woods, it is in your imagination. So you lie back down, feeling sleepy. You whisper yes's to yourself that last more than five minutes; then, with the scarecrow standing guard, you fall asleep.

But even a Friday-tired, Seconalled sleep doesn't last long. So you wake shortly thereafter and walk back to the trailer, where the indoor campground awaits you. Sleeping bags.

Yet you don't feel like camping out anywhere, so you begin to get dressed to go into the city. The Seconal is tearing you up, and you stumble around until you finally get your boots on.

In the mirror, you no longer feel beautiful. Still, you stand there for the longest time.

Standing guard.

Zachary found New York to be the loneliest place in the world. During the two years he lived there he felt that he was constantly scattering pieces of himself all around the city, forgetting to keep a checklist. If he had kept more notes, maybe he wouldn't have found himself going so far east, so far into the dark, to places where doors slammed shut as beautiful night-crawlers went down on lines of coke like anxious pigs. Only the coke was more bitter. That's when he met the painter, Carlos. At one of these places so far in the East Village that walking through the door was like stepping off a tightrope. He was with his friend Jessica at such a place on Avenue B when he met the painter. The Colombian painter looked like a meatier Johnny Thunders come back to life. At first he thought that the painter was straight; maybe this was because of the way that the kissing started between Jessica and him; then suddenly they were all kissing. Then Carlos was kissing Zachary more, and then more. "We want coke," Zachary said, not knowing the golden explosive mine he'd just discovered.

Carlos' apartment was like love. With a winding staircase, beautiful paintings, a huge bed where Jessica passed out. Then they started. That was the first time they did coke together.

And it was a beautiful thing, though Zachary was disappointed that the coke made them too limp to fuck. And sunrise came three hours later, but it felt like only a few minutes had passed since he and Jessica had fallen into the bar.

The painter loved him, this he knew. And there would be the nightly begging for Zachary to stay, but sometimes when Zachary would look at the painter, he would see the professor. And it was enough to make the beautiful Colombian features of Carlos become horrific. And when the painter opened his mouth to kiss Zachary, sticking his tongue in was like slipping into a lion's mouth. He'd been eaten alive before, but somehow the coke and the vodka straight up, made it all seem like danger was the way to go.

"You know what I do besides paint?"

"Tell me." *This was one night after they'd done at least a gram and cried over Allen Ginsberg's "Death & Fame" poem in the* New Yorker.

"I deal drugs." *Carlos said, nervously taking a sip of his vodka, as if he had just revealed something that Zachary didn't already know.*

"It's fine...," *Zachary said.*

And it was, as Zachary got up to a gram and half a day of free coke. He felt like a cliché out of an eighties novel, but as he began to go from skinny to bones, he realized that situations like this were never clichéd.

"Call in sick for me today," *he'd tell Carlos, on days too numerous to count. And still half-asleep, he'd hear Carlos say in broken English,* "Zachary's sick. He can't work."

Standing became a problem sometimes, and hunger eluded him. Food was a drug to him now. Everything lost its flavor; it was all like paper. And if it was spicy, it was like cough syrup. It always made him want to break dishes or just set it on the floor and let the cat eat it up, along with the coke it had found from the night before.

The weaker he got, the more ceilings took on lives of their own. Not only Carlos' but the one in Zachary's own small apartment he'd taken to get away from the professor. Zach-

ary's apartment always felt dusty, uncleanable. The ceiling had holes in it, like some sort of upside-down strainer, and when it rained, he'd have to place buckets around the room. Sometimes, in that room, he'd sit in the dark watching the raindrops by the light of a single lit candle. It looked like the rain was rising up from the mismatched buckets — a room full of geysers, the water gushing its way up from the dusty floor.

The phone would ring on these occasions. People from school, people from back home. Worried people. And since he was worried, too, he couldn't even talk to them. He didn't want to say anything because he felt embarrassed for the cliché which he knew he was destined to become. And he certainly couldn't let them see him, looking like a skeleton. He was glad March was still cold so that he could at least wear layers of clothes when he had to go out.

He was only okay at Carlos' these days. "My beautiful junkie" somehow sounded good, because nobody had ever called him beautiful before. He could ignore the junkie part. Beside the fact that they were dying together from this combination of liquor, cocaine, and sunrises that always blindingly shocked them, there were some good moments. Reading poetry, talking about everything from vacations and exotic places to artistic success was what kept them alive. But the only actual resort was tucked in the East Village, which was filled with artifacts from India and Columbia. The soundtrack to the movie that Zachary found himself moving through was not bad. Van Morrison, Bob Dylan, and The Stones. "Lady Jane" was the theme of that rainy winter's end. At least the ceiling in Carlos' apartment was sturdier than Zachary's. He didn't have to worry about anything coming down on him at night or slipping up through the cracks that he always feared he'd be sucked down through in his own apartment.

One night, after he refused to spend the night because he was afraid to have sex, knowing that Carlos had been exposed to all those diseases he'd read too much about to ever enjoy loving him the way he wanted to, Carlos grew angry. "Well, can I have a bag for tomorrow?" This had seemed greedy in the *beginning, but now it had become a ritual.*

"No. Get out. If you want to stay with me, then stay. Or else it's over."

He left, shaking from all the coke with no Valium, no sleeping pills, to take the edge off. He wondered how he'd work the next day. He didn't want to go back to his apartment, so at some brightly lit car wash on Houston Street, he stopped at a pay phone. In the silver of the phone, he saw how the formation of death had begun to take shape in his sunken cheeks and a complexion that only real ghosts could overlook. He dialed the number. It was now 5 a.m. "Girgio?"

"Yes."

"It's Zachary. Can I come home?"

"No."

He slept in the park that night, not wanting to sleep in his apartment ever again. He went to the bank and got a cash advance and called an old friend who delivered him two grams of coke. He didn't even really want it. It was just what he did now.

He sat in his apartment for the rest of the day, dialing all of the airlines to find the cheapest fare, then realized that they were all basically the same. So he maxed out the credit card that night. He left most of his stuff in the apartment, didn't call anybody, and flew south, drinking all the way there, wondering why he was even going back. But knowing the city was actually killing him, he found himself calming down, enjoying being in the air this way, pretending that the plane would never stop drifting through the air.

28

There he is. After you have taken your silver keys from the coffee table, you see him standing in the open doorway, a gorgeousness of bones and messy blond hair. The Seconal brings slow blinks to the lids of your eyes; his presence stalls you. Stunning arrivals. And pleasant ambush. You are not sure what the words would be if you uttered them. They are swimming around inside of you, an internal flood of disconnected sentences.

"Hello" is all that you can say. All of those things that you've ever been saving up to say come in that single world which everyone understands, but knows means nothing. Like with Gina, you can't say what you feel. Unreleased. You stagger a little closer to him, not understanding why you are at a loss for words. He is no longer a stranger, and you feel things for him that Gina never brought out of you.

"Can I come in?" You picture him in many cities, lying in darkened rooms screaming to get out.

"Disappearer," you say, not angrily, but with a slur. Then you have one of your drunken moments, where you secretly tell yourself this is a big deal and you'd better sober up some. "Of course, come in." You move clumsily to the couch, fold the afghan, and throw it across the back of the chair.

When he passes by you in his T-shirt and jeans, you want to reach out and grab him by one of his arms. Arms so thin that you can wrap your entire fist around them and hug him like that. Circulation. You open the window. "I got your letter," you tell him.

"I guess it was pretty silly. It's one of those things you drop in the mailbox and then realize that you've just done something as revealing as walking through town naked."

145

"Little disappearer," you say, slapping him gently on the leg. You can feel him twitching through the denim. In his face, you see the wide-awake exhausted signs that he's been playing the game again. Straws, powder. "Fucked up?" you actually ask him.

"A little. You?"

"Some. Do you want a drink?" You ask this, knowing he needs something to take the edge off. He is wired to the point where you can almost see the ends of his hair move. Dusted electrification.

"Got anything stronger? I think I did too much. Again. That room just got to me after a while, so I went to Hattiesburg and scored, then went to the field."

You give him a Seconal and get up to pour him a glass of water. You are so glad he's here, but hate the way he was missing for so long. "M-I-A," you say loudly going back to the living room.

"I guess so."

"How come I didn't hear you in the field? Just because of the cops?"

"I don't wanna go back to jail." He shakes his head. "Those cops, man. They really hate me."

"Why you?"

"Because I'm a fag. I never was a boy that liked to skin deer. Once when I was twenty, one of them asked me if I had 'gone the way of the homos.' I told him yes. It's been hell ever since."

Both of you are kicked back on the couch, your feet on the coffee table, almost touching. Two things Gina didn't take. "Why do you stay? Why did you return?"

"Because my roots are here. I feel like I belong here in a way that sometimes I need to remind myself of. When listening to music. That's when it all makes sense. The reason why I came back from New York, the reason that I'm gay, why I'm even alive." He pauses for a moment, and at first it seems like he's not going to continue, but he does. "You know, I'm not one of those people that think there's a reason for everything. But when I'm in that field, I feel there is a reason for it. It's like, if there really was such a thing as God or somebody like that, that's where they'd want me to be."

You watch as he plays with his glass nervously, as if he's sipping a fine brandy. You reach over and touch his hair. He is calmer now. "Are you afraid of some of the people in his town?"

"I'm afraid of everybody," he laughs. It take you a few seconds to realize it's okay for you to laugh, too. "You know, there is always something to fear. In New York, well, it was someone. In Paris, it was not knowing the language, and here it's the cops and the Christians."

"I'll go to the field with you," you tell him. "We can take sleeping bags out there."

"I don't know."

Now you realize that he's scared of you, too. Sometimes it's hard to believe he's twenty-six. "Don't worry, Zachary. I'm not going to touch you like that. It might just be nice to be out there where you belong. It's where you want to be."

"Okay," he whispers.

He follows you into the bedroom where you take two sleeping bags from the closet. You realize now that Gina did leave something useful behind.

"Don't you have a bed?" he wonders.

"No, not anymore, not since the separation."

He studies the bedroom's emptiness as though he doesn't want to leave it. "I've spent a lot of my days in darkened rooms, too," you let him know. "It's not a place we should be." Still, he takes in the space some more. Finally he follows you down the hall.

As you exit the trailer, he seems pleased with the idea of a grassy night. "You like dark fields, too?" he asks.

"Sometimes I love them, but sometimes they are like bedrooms."

As you cross the highway, you realize that you've never heard Zachary talk so much. But as you near the scarecrow he is quieter. You want to tell Zachary stories. You want to tell him about the time you got separated from your platoon and stayed up all night as the other side moved in. But the silence seems so right that you let the story rest.

He is yawning as you spread the sleeping bags out. The scarecrow will once again watch over you and Zachary. Night watchers like him never sleep.

He immediately crawls into the dark red sleeping bag, yawning again. "I'm glad you came over," you let him know.

Sitting on your blue bag, you hold your knees in your hands, wanting to be holding him, but afraid to. Afraid you'll squeeze too hard. Fragility.

Lying there, his eyes look barely open. He talks slowly, dreamily. "You know, once there were these two French poets," he drags out. "Do you know poetry?"

"No." This honesty makes you feel stupid.

"They were in love, and one of them left the other behind in Paris. And the one that was left went to the pier and screamed that he loved the other one to the whole world."

He's drowsy now, and you're not sure if he's dreaming this or if it's actually true. You choose to believe it as history.

"Like the field," he mumbles, "given over to oblivion...growing with incense and and wild grass."

"Did you just make that up?"

He grins on the verge of sleeping-pill heaven. "I wish. Benjamin Britten understood those words."

"I don't know who that is," you tell him.

"Yes," he says, "you do. You've heard it all before from the field." A car passes slowly along the road. "If I have a taste, it is for the earth and stones..." He seems drunk with his poetry.

"I didn't know where you were," you tell him, trying to get him to come back to life as it is now. You wish you hadn't given him the Seconal. He's in a dream world, as you hold your own body. "I said I didn't know where you were."

"I always fed on air..."

"Zachary," you finally bring yourself to say, "I think you're beautiful."

But he is sleeping. Gone away again. You feel a wetness trying to seep from your eyes, but nothing much comes out. He has left again, and even if you went to sleep, you couldn't catch up with him and his dreams. He is far away. Missing in action.

The night is getting colder, and he is sighing gently with each second.

When it starts to drizzle, you don't want to wake him, and one of those moments occurs where the field becomes a place of the past. The scarecrow becomes nearly ominous. The lightning in the distance makes you shake. You listen carefully, making sure that he is still breathing; then, like you did with bodies days long ago, you pick him up. You grab both sleeping bags. His hits the ground, but you leave it. It doesn't need to be carried the way Zachary does.

He mumbles something as you carry him to the trailer. You are blinded by some bright light from down the road and circles dance in front of your eyes as you enter the trailer.

In the bedroom, you think about putting him in your sleeping bag, but you change your mind. Body bags, suffocation. Instead you lay him on the couch. Then somehow you find the energy to drag Lula's tattered mattress into the living room. You throw a lime-colored sheet and a couple of pillows at the head of it.

The rain is just barely falling outside. After you've put him on the mattress, he stirs, mumbling in tongues you wish you could understand. You want to hear everything he has to say. But right now he is a prisoner of his deep, dreamy sleep.

You take another sleeping pill and wash it down with a small shot of bourbon. Then you lie beside him, the rain sounding musical. It makes you think of The Association song, "Cherish." Even the thunder is pleasant, and every time lightning streaks through the room, you watch it turn your dumpy trailer into a disco for a second or two.

You assume that you'll fall asleep soon, so you lie back, staring at him, realizing how perfect the left hoop looks in his ear and how you want to touch it. Dog tags have never looked so good on a civilian. Instead of touching him, you begin to feel drowsy and find yourself getting lost with him, on your way to missing in action in a world of dreams. The sleep comes on slowly, then all at once.

Soon you are lost in the same cage of soft sighs and sharp images.

Prisoners of war.

29

You two sleep through dawn, through the afternoon, and you awake at 6 p.m. the following night, confused by the darkness. He is still sleeping. You hear the storm roaring away. The slight drizzle has turned violent. When you get up to get a glass of orange juice, you cannot see. There is something wrong. The light switches don't work, the refrigerator is off. Unelectrified. The storm outside has led to a power outage.

You light the oil lamp that always sits on the television. You haven't slept so deeply since you were in the hospital. You look outside, knowing that Richard must be livid at not being able to work. The scarecrow is rocking slightly in the wind. And if you look at it in just the right way, it seems to be walking either slowly forward or backward, but you can't tell which.

A storm is a beautiful thing to you, because it puts no pressure on you to be all right. It is okay to be confused, deranged, exuberant, or sad during a storm. As you listen to the roaring weather, you try to recall some of your dreams, but none of them come back. The sleep was that deep.

"What time is it?" He asks this as you continue to stare out the window.

"It's tomorrow," you say. "Tomorrow night. We slept through the whole day. And the lights are out because of the storm."

You don't look at him because it is too hard not to touch him. But you do hear him moving around, his dog tags clanging, the snap of his jeans, the zipper, a shirt sliding up and off. "Please...," he says, though you're still not looking at him.

"I don't want to hurt you," you inform him.

"I know now that you won't."

You turn to him, wanting every bone of his to belong to only you and him. He looks puffy around the eyes, but they glisten, blinding you like the earlier lightning. You slip off your shirt and slip your paint-stained khakis farther and farther down until they are no longer on you. He is watching this from the mattress, where he seems to be covering himself with his long arms, like suddenly he's changed his mind and doesn't want to be seen. Another disappearance.

The way he looks at your tan body, wrapped only in your white briefs, is the look you have been craving from somebody for years. Somebody like him. Not since the war has somebody looked at you and without saying a word told you that they like what they saw.

"Can we turn out the lamp?" he asks, still covering himself.

"Why?"

"I know I'm not like those guys. I don't look like them."

"What guys?"

"You know, the poster boys, the ones who are not bones wrapped in skin."

"I want to see you. You are all of those things, Zachary. You were made to live in light. You are my poster boy. Don't you ever look in the mirror?"

"No." He lets out a nervous laugh and covers his mouth, obviously not wanting to show his teeth.

You take this beautiful boy by the hand and make him face the television screen. From behind, you wrap your arms around him. "Beautiful," you say. "I love your teeth," you tell him honestly. "Beautiful."

He begins to grow hard, larger and thicker than you expected. It is the only fat thing about him, and you love it.

He turns to face you, seeming less shy, all yours, wanting it that way. "My scarecrow...," you say, before falling to your knees. You take him as deep in your throat as possible and look up as he closes his eyes, sighing like during his sleep. He tastes good—not only better than any other you've ever sucked, but he somehow fits perfectly into your mouth. The fat straightness has found a home.

You don't want him to come yet, so you pull away and fall back onto the mattress, letting him tear your white underwear away as you begin to rock slowly and softly into his mouth. You moan as he sucks away any bad thoughts.

"Fuck me," you say before he has the chance to.

"I don't have a condom."

"Fuck me anyway." You ignore his statement. Shields of rubber, warfare.

He rolls you over and tastes you in that delicate space you want him to plunge himself into; it is like he's never tasted an asshole before. And you've never been had this way. It will hurt, you want it to. So when you feel him rubbing his spit all over your hole, your dick begins to dance anxiously.

Two of his long fingers go in and rip at you, a warning of what will come. You touch your cock, jerking it only a little. You know that he is big, and that his fingers are probably like nothing at all.

And you are right. A sound comes from your throat as he enters you. The thunder is defeated by your groans as he drives slowly into you once. It feels as if his dick will come out of your bellybutton at any moment. Twice. It hurts. You like this pain, not because you feel that you deserve it, but because, unlike a gunshot, you asked for it.

And by the sixth stroke it is almost pleasurable. He is jamming more swiftly now, leaving you to bite the pillow, pleasantly paralyzed from the bottom up. You move your ass back a little and deeper he goes. His penetration is fierce, then slow, then fast again. He is killing you and bringing you alive at the same time. Now you want it all. Harder.

"Fuck me," you sigh. Though it doesn't seen possible for him to go any deeper, he somehow finds a way to. You feel him ready to shoot and blow your insides away.

It is as if you've never had an ass before. Your balls are churning. You want to shoot and be shot at the same time.

His mouth is on the back of your neck, when you feel him drive you to the point where you can't keep it bottled up any longer.

Your whiteness hits the sheets as he burns you up with a shot of himself, collapsing on top of you, holding tightly. "You are beautiful, too," he says to you, words that you've needed to hear from him since the first time you met. "I love to hold onto you like this," he tells you.

The bones of his chest are pressed firmly against your back. You stay like this forever. The world has become a new place.

Before he slowly gets out of you, there is a clicking noise. It is the refrigerator and the lamp coming on. Light.

You lie there, together, bones against bones. It is then that you notice your bottle of Valium slipped out of your pocket and is scattered all over the mattress. You see one sticking to his arm and several are stuck to your chest. Instead of taking one, you hold onto each other. Bones matching, fitting perfectly into place. This all frightens away the bluebirds known as Valium.

Scarecrows.

Zachary noticed that each time he made love to somebody, they'd put their hand over his mouth during sex. At first he thought it was because he was too noisy. So he began to silence himself. Then one night, completely without uttering a word, a guy from Brooklyn kept forcing his mouth closed.

Then there were the professor's wisecracks about his gap-toothed grin, Carlos' accurate portraits of Zachary's enormous mouth with fucked-up teeth inside. These were the later ones. He wanted braces when he was a boy.

At twenty-five, he didn't want braces anymore. When he finally got the money to go get some work done on his teeth, the dentist even seemed overwhelmed. "You're never going to have a Hollywood smile," the dentist said frankly.

Zachary learned to keep his mouth closed, tossing photographs of his monstrous grin away. When he met people he'd first talk looking down, then after he knew that they were okay no matter what his mouth looked like, he opened it wider and began to talk to them instead of the floor.

One night, at a party, when he had too much to drink and the bad performance art reached a point of ridiculousness that even the performers must have been embarrassed by, something happened.

It happened while the professor was lost in a crowd of people who called themselves artists and really meant it. A woman, stunning, came and sat next to him on a comfortable sofa in a dark corner. He thought she was a famous model, and she may have been. But he was too drunk to know for sure. "You are really cute," she said. "Really cute." Her accent was British, and her hair was the blondest he'd ever seen. Then she leaned over and she kissed him

"If you had good teeth, you could be really beautiful," she said.

And her saying that was like she had never kissed him. "I know a great dentist," she said.

He was silent. Her pleasant words were hurting him, and he was sure she was trying to be helpful. But at the moment, after too many shots of Goldschläger, he felt like the ugliest person at the party, which was full of some of the strangest people he had ever seen. He stood up.

"I didn't mean..." The British voice trailed off.

He went to look for the professor. But the crowd was thick; people were watching a man in drag shouting "Isis" over and over again to the point where the silliness almost sobered Zachary up. And the crowd seemed to be completely *enthralled. When he looked away, he felt woozy, beyond drunk. Too much as always.*

He found his way to the bathroom. The mirrors were brutal in their honesty. He felt short at the moment, as if he was standing on the basin looking at his reflection. But then his head became enormous, and now he knew what the professor meant when he used to say his forehead was the biggest he'd ever seen. Slowly he opened his mouth, which seemed to cover his entire face.

Now he really looked at his teeth. They were a sight, the front two with a space big enough to floss with a rope. And the others, pointed and not quite where they belonged. He studied them more. His mouth grew wider.

He could get his hair cut just the right way to cover the forehead, he could wear tons of clothes to cover his thinness, he could wear colored contacts to make his eyes more blue. But the teeth were beyond repair. And he began to grow angry, almost wishing they'd all fall out. He was wanting to be reborn, to have a normal set of teeth that were at least fixable. He didn't expect the most beautiful teeth in the world, just average ones like most people had or paid to have.

He must have kept his mouth open for a good five minutes, and in a rage of anger and solitude, he opened up even farther. His mouth became his face. Feeling part-vampire, part-werewolf, a little Frankenstein, he let out a noise. A loud noise. He howled at the top of his lungs. His mouth was open so fiercely, every muscle being used, that he knew that nobody, no matter how strong their hands were, could force it shut.

People must have heard him, because a gang of them rushed into the bathroom. Some of them were in latex, some wore jeans. And they just stared at him as he turned around. He saw it in their faces that he'd caused another scene. Zachary was drunk again. But he stared back at them, his mouth still open. He wasn't going to shut it for them.

Had he done it on the stage where everyone was probably still engrossed in the performer, he would have been considered brilliant. After he finally found the professor and they went *home for a nice quick fuck, he bit down on his shoulder, drawing blood. This pleased the professor. He'd make the teeth work for him, painting something very abstract by placing hickeys all over the professor's body.*

30

It continues to rain Thursday and Friday, and you spend both days rolling around on the mattress thrown across the living room floor. Things good like this happen so rarely that you know you better just let them occur. The two of you order pizza, and talk, and tumble around on a bed of surprisingly uneaten Valium and spilled cocaine. The coke feels like rough sand against your naked bodies. These substances are not your life as much as they were last week or the week before. Even the bottle of Jack Daniel's sits with the lid off, half-full.

This is the longest you've ever gone naked. You don't put on clothes until Saturday afternoon when Zachary says he wants to see a movie. He's been talking about this movie in an obsessive way. And you love him for it, because it makes you excited about things you used to never give a second thought to.

All the way there, he talks about it. "It's about words; subtitles are perfect for this movie. It's about a factory worker in Italy who falls in love with his brother's wife, and she teaches him how to write."

"How many times have you seen it?" you ask, seeing the Catfish Shack on the horizon.

"Just once. Movies like this don't last long around here. It's like reading poetry. But more..."

The parking lot is full of everybody in Petulia on a Saturday night. As you walk toward the movie theater, something strange happens. Slow-motion. Having everyone stare at you is like trudging through mud. You knew that people would already be talking about this thing with Zachary, but not so soon. And you do care because you feel surrounded, shot over and over again by eyes. You want to turn and go back home. But when you look at him and the way he moves, beautifully, perfectly paced, you try to follow. He doesn't walk slow like you. His colorful braveness is admirable.

People still stare, making you wish you'd taken a Valium. Empty pill pockets are a new thing to you. A couple in front of you giggle. You are sure she is a Wal-Mart cashier. If she's not, she will be someday. Everyone is turning to stare at you. It's as if they don't even think you are Gary Slope any longer. It is like high school all over again, and you feel like one of the uncool people, and this makes you feel ashamed.

Zachary looks calm until he sees your nervousness. On the spot, you wonder if maybe nobody is talking about you at all. Most of them are going to see a disaster movie, just like the one they saw last week. You pull your sweater around you tighter as it grows cooler. Zachary is hidden behind his oversized red-and-blue-striped pullover, covering everything including his hands. You think that when people look at you, they can see how Zachary fucked you until you screamed.

You get your tickets and begin to button your sweater just to look busy. "It's gonna be good," he says. "I always end up seeing movies alone. Thank you for coming with me."

You manage a smile, knowing he deserves more. Like an arm around his waist or your hands in one another's. Allies. Maybe you were never a good soldier. Not like him.

You wait by the entrance to theater six, while he buys popcorn and the biggest Coke ever poured. Even while he is at the concession stand you feel everyone in the theater is like the scarecrow. They can see it all. It seems like they can see how you ground and rocked each other naked for two days straight.

But for brief moments, when he comes toward you, with the immense popcorn and Coke, you forget that other people are even around. The blue in his pullover makes his skin look just pale enough. And his eyes shift from green to blue, then back again.

There is only one other couple in the theater where this foreign film is showing. You make your way to the back row; he follows, then disappears. He's taken a seat in the center of the place. "I don't want to sit all the way back there," he says, "I won't."

You tug at the bottom of your sweater and sit down beside him.

"This is too hard for you?" he says in an asking sort of way.

"Yes."

"You can leave."

"No."

The lights go down. Previews of movies you know he likes. "I want to see that one," he whispers after each trailer.

You take some of the popcorn, greedily, like you took him on the mattress.

In Vietnam, you missed going to movies so much that you'd sometimes dream complete scripts, none of which you ever remembered for long. But after you returned to the States, you stopped dreaming in movies and never dreamed complete scripts again.

More people file in. You want to enjoy this for him. A young couple sits behind you. As the Italian music starts, they whisper. "Faggots," one of them says. You look at Zachary, who closes his eyes as though he's sick, then opens them looking as healthy as ever. He tosses his anger with a blink. Letting go.

In the darkness, you read the movie, and it moves at the same pace as you had when entering the theater. It is the type of movie that you dreamed up in Vietnam. One with a kind of language where a single word could mean more than an entire sentence.

There is something about the darkness of the theater and the sad music that leads you to take his hand. As the frail Italian actor counts in Italian, you look at Zachary and his glassy eyes. You squeeze his hand as greedily as you've ever squeezed anything. Just like earlier, he opens and closes his small eyes with relief.

You don't let go of him through the rest of the movie. Faggots.

When the lights go up, the two of you sit still. His eyes are glassy as he runs the tips of his fingers along his full bottom lip. Gorgeous. How could you have been embarrassed?

He sits there, not moving until after the theater has completely cleared out and the screen is black. Entranced.

"Why did you do it?"

"Take my hand?"

"Because I wanted to hold your hand the way you taught me to."

He is still not crying, but you can tell that he is close to it.

"I'm sorry about those people," you tell him. "I'm sorry for what they called us. Don't cry, scarecrow, they're assholes."

He laughs hard. "I'm used to them. It's the movie I'm sad over." He jabs you with his elbow. His skin seems softly bulletproof. "Great film," he says. "What time is it?"

"*Dieci.*"

"Good, now let's go to Waffle House for food. Everybody goes there. That way, everyone will have something to talk about tomorrow."

He stands and marches to the exit. A real soldier, you think. Of honor. You follow, wanting to be on his side.

31

Back home, you end up like this. Something new. A deeper way of making love to him, of really giving it to him. He is tight, so when you enter him he claws at the couch. You've never done it to him before. His left knee is on the carpet, his right leg stretched out along the couch. You drive into him trying to make up for your earlier behavior, wanting to go deeper than before. Promising with each thrust of your hips that you'll never behave that way again. Each time you are with him, you will hold him close. Pride.

Strong words come before coming. "I love you," you whisper. You are bringing your balls to a churning that matches your own. The deeper you go, the more he sucks you into his small but perfectly round ass. He is your scarecrow, but bulging in all the right places.

Grunts. Unleashing, slamming against him as he falls across the couch. He doesn't mind if the lights are on now. In fact, he seems to like you seeing his body.

You think about having a sip of the whiskey, which is sitting there, ready to be guzzled. But making love to Zachary makes you want to continue the sober ritual you began days ago.

Part of the ritual is like this. Organic orange juice in wine glasses after the loving. The house is feeling like a home again. The kitchen no longer feels like a place that is only good for sharp butcher knives and hidden bottles of potent pills and liquors.

He is lying flat on the mattress when you return, looking tired, looking like he'll remain loved for a while. He sits up, and you fall beside him. You raise your glasses. A toast.

"To this night," you proclaim.

"Cheers."

"Waffle House is so straight," he says, "I can't believe we went there."

"It was your idea."

"I know, but I used to work there as a cook once," he says, finishing his orange juice. He lies back down, his arms folding behind his head, his dog tag glowing against his chest. "They fired me, of course. But once I blew a Texas truck driver there in the bathroom."

"How was it?" You're a little jealous and put your empty glass on the floor beside you.

"It was nothing," he says. "I thought it was, but now I know what something really is. We're something. But I like to go to Waffle House to cut the edge," he tells you. "For over twenty years, I've been invisible in this town. I want them to see me. Not to show off, just to let them know that I'm here."

"The autumn Southern soldier," you say, pulling him close. You feel his body becoming more sleepy, each part becoming more sleepy. You should let him rest.

"Gary?"

"Yes?"

"Would you love me even if I was dying? Even if I was dead?"

"Even in death," you say, a little worried. "Why do you ask?"

"Because that's how I love you."

You kiss him on the cheek as he falls asleep.

You haven't taken one of the scattered Valium in a long while, and see one stuck to his arm. You stare at its small pale blue roundness, hoping just seeing it will put you to sleep. Then you see the bottle of whiskey and reach for it, wanting only a bit. But when you move to get it, it falls and spills into a perfect stream onto the carpet. Waterfalls. It make you think of a time when you would have never been so careless as to waste a drop.

You let it spill completely. Then you turn back over to this boy who knows how to be held. This time when you stare at the Valium still stuck to his arm, it makes you yawn.

It can't be more than thirty minutes when you've started a really vivid dream about being a black man, bound by silk ties to a brass bed. Then you are awakened by the lights. They are coming from the window again. At first you think it's a car, but no car ever flashed like this. Not even cops.

Like you, Zachary rises, and watches as you move to the window, blinded by the lights whose origins are unknown.

He is scared and wraps himself in the blanket. It is a light so bright that you can practically hear it. It sounds like a scream.

"Don't worry," you assure him. "It's probably just a car turning around."

"It's something else. It's too bright."

Then it is gone. "See," you assure him. "Happens all the time. Lay down. Sleep."

He moves his back into your belly. Spoons.

32

The Sunday sun wakes you up too early to rise on a day off. On your way to the bathroom, a Valium that has stuck to your side falls to the carpet. You don't reach down to pick it up. The desire is there as always, but it's too much trouble.

As you pee, the bathroom mirror doesn't make you hate what you see in it. Today could be a handsome day. In the living room, you sit on the couch and the wind blows in the through the window, that coolness that you like. You cover him with the paisley comforter and wrap yourself in the afghan. You are content to be awake this Sunday, and when the birds come to the window, you watch them waiting for you to throw them some bread. You realize that you've never thought about feeding a bird your entire life, and have certainly never considered building a birdhouse. The room smells like whiskey, which you spilled so accidentally on purpose last night.

There are more birds today than usual. Their music wakes Zachary. You watch as his fingers move across your pillow in search of somebody you're glad is you.

He is soon next to you. "Why are you up so early?" he wants to know, yawning.

"Can you believe I've never fed a bird?" you say.

"You mean no matter how skinny or sad they looked, you never fed them?" You can tell he is still sleepy, his eyes puffy like he didn't even go to bed. You are sure he'll wind up falling asleep during the day. "When I build scarecrows, I try to not make them too scary. There's no corn out there, anyway. I don't want to scare them. But you mean to tell me, you've never ever fed a bird?"

"Never."

"Not even in the park?"

"No."

"I don't believe you."

"It's true."

You can tell by how he almost ignores you that he still can't quite believe it. "We can feed them now," he says. "Our way."

You watch as he takes a bowl that he had cereal in the night before and fills it with the small bottle of vodka to see birds fly higher than normal. "I always had the feeling that they could go higher." He picks several Valium up from the floor and tosses them out onto the ground.

"Are you still sleeping?" you ask.

"Yes, pretty much." He hands you a few pills and you surprise yourself by following his behavior.

You watch as the birds stare suspiciously at their breakfast, then one by one they begin to eat them. Some of them getting more than others. The vodka they won't touch, so Zachary gets them a bowl of water. You pick up more pills and throw them out, amazed that you are doing this, watching birds fight over something that you are sure will kill them.

"Why are we doing this?" you ask.

"Let's see how high they go." He moves closer to you. "Get under the comforter with me." You don't want to disappoint him by telling him that the birds will never leave the ground.

"I used to be afraid of birds," he says.

"Is that why you just killed so many?"

"I don't know," he says, rubbing his eyes, leaning against you. "I never was one to go hunting, never could shoot a gun."

"I guess you're making up for it now."

"Maybe..."

He still needs more sleep, and you want him to get it soon. You don't want him to witness the drunken birds keel over. You channel-flip through the morning news shows as he begins to sleep again.

When you look out, you are amazed to see the first of the birds take off. And then in sync, suddenly, more like a swarm of sober bees. You wait for them to fall, but you run to the front door. "Zachary, come see!"

He gets to the door as soon as his grogginess allows him to. But by then they have all ascended beyond sight. "They fucking flew. I never saw birds fly so high!"

"I told you," he says, not surprised at all. "Will you come back to bed with me?" he asks.

You agree to do this, because some more sleep would do you good. After all, tomorrow you will start work on a new house. Beneath the covers your limbs touch. Sometimes it is hard to tell which arms and legs belong to you and which are his.

It doesn't matter. His and his.

33

Gina calls early, sounding like there is fire in her voice. "Gary?"

"Gina, it's seven o'clock in the morning."

"Unbelievable. I heard the rumors, I didn't want to believe them. I was such a fool." She's crying. This is only the eye of the storm, you figure. "How could you? How?"

You want to tell her to take a pair of your shoes from 1974 and try to walk in them for so many years. But she has a right to be this angry, so you let her go on.

You know her so well that you can see her standing there, shaking with the receiver in her hand. "Everybody knows about you and him." You imagine her shrinking and floating around in the fish tank she took, coming up for air, breathing and not yelling.

"Well, aren't you going to say something?" she asks.

Zachary is stirring now. "You've already said it all."

"Always the quiet one. Can't you speak to me for once? Even now, can't you have a talk with me?" There is silence; you let her go on. "Do you know what it's like for me and Eddie. The humiliation. He was thinking of running for sheriff, but now... And I can't even go to the store without people whispering. Can you imagine what that's like for me?"

"Yes, I can."

"But you got yourself into this. Us into this." She is really crying now. Sobbing. You can picture her beautiful face streaming with tears, knowing she has every right to make you feel the guilt swell up.

"There is no us."

"And the stupid thing is that I still love you."

You love her, too, but saying this could be dangerous.

"Have you been outside today? Have you seen the

outside of the trailer? I was driving down the road, trying not to think about any of these rumors and the humiliation, and I passed the trailer and those big red letters just caught my eye. Letters bigger than life itself were printed all over the front."

"What are you talking about?"

Zachary has walked up and wrapped his arms around you. "Just go outside and look. You'll see how bad it's gotten," she cries. "Goodbye, Gary."

"Well, I guess we're awake now," you joke.

You lead him outside, both of you only in your briefs in the way-too-cold morning. Shivering, you read the letters that cover the front of the trailer. Q-U-E-E-R.

For a second you wait for a tornado to pick the trailer up and send it to another land. Then you remember how people used to spray-paint various things all over buildings in Saigon. So you go to your truck. Zachary seems more shocked than you by the graffiti. He stands, his arms folded, his mouth half-opened.

"They forgot something," you say, taking a can of spray-paint from the floorboard of the truck.

And on the far right where there is just enough room for another letter you add an *S*. It stands out, almost overpowering the other letters.

As you throw the can back into the truck, you catch your reflection in the rearview mirror, which you still haven't fixed completely. Today could be a handsome day after all.

34

Now when you watch *60 Minutes*, the clock seems to be moving in the right direction. It is around the half-hour point of the show when Zachary first notices what else has happened.

You hear him calling out from the field. At first it sounds like him, then like hundreds of Zacharies. From the window, you see him standing in the dusky field, dropping to his knees as the book of poetry he is reading falls from his hand. And like with Will jumping from the Wal-Mart, you see him fall again and again. He isn't yelling anything in particular, simply bellowing out as if you can understand him without specific words. Minds read.

Once you reach the field, you hear him wailing as if someone has died.

"Where's the scarecrow?"

"It was amazing. It disappeared."

"Oh, Zachary, come on..."

"I swear. It just went away."

You place a hand on Zachary's shoulder. "You can make another one."

"No," he warns you, sounding more childlike than usual. "That is not true."

"Zachary, come back inside."

"No. Not yet, I want to be out here."

He is breathing hard as you walk away. Since they took away his opera, he is creating his own passionate music from somewhere within his chest. It's hard for you to walk away from a young man who's upset. But this time it is for him. It is a way that only someone who could see life out of a scarecrow's eyes could understand.

Then you flash, this time farther back. You remember sobbing for grown men, some dying, some just afraid that they were going to.

Inside, the *60 Minutes* clock seems to be moving backward like it used to. You don't want to be like a hand on that clock. But the floor begins to bend as you walk across it, searching for any pill, knowing that if you saw a bird now, any bird, you'd strangle it for having fed on your food.

Outside there are sobs, then you hear marching. When you look out there, you are amazed at what you see. Zachary is lying on his back staring at the sky. You turn away, afraid that seeing any more of this will make the noises you heard earlier return. Knowing that he will not make it inside before the enemies arrive. You still hear them coming. You begin to throw things around the room, going crazy for the first time in over a month. You smash an old bluegrass album into a million pieces.

You put on some music from Zachary's collection and crank it as loud as it will go, drowning out the sounds of the war which has made its way home.

"Will you love me even when I'm dead?" you remember him asking.

You are blasting something operatic by Britten. Still, once in a while you can hear explosions outside. The trailer feels like cellophane.

You dig for pills but all of the bottles are empty, the liquor all drained. You wonder where the birds went. After you've exhausted yourself from digging for things you know are gone, you collapse onto the couch.

The music suddenly grows lower. "I could hear it all the way out there," he tells you, red-eyed but calm now as he turns the stereo down. He throws his book onto the floor and holds the yellow tie that used to be wrapped around the scarecrow's neck.

Seeing him makes the darkness become more gray than black, the shaking washes away. This time he comes to you. "It's gone," he says. "Don't you believe me. It just disappeared."

"I know." You feel good to find your mind return-ing, hoping that you didn't do anything as horrendous as you have in your past. His hands take yours, and they bring sobriety in the form of sanity. This time he is the one that takes you into his arms. Only moments ago, you saw him grabbing at the earth, untouchable by human hands. And now he holds you in a way that make his blue T-shirt seem more brilliant. The way he rubs his hand along your spine turns the trailer into a home again.

He holds you for the longest time, rocking you as if you were the scarecrow. As if you had just had your head chopped off. "I heard you in here, yelling louder than the music," he says to your left ear. Breath.

"You should have heard yourself," you say.

"I couldn't."

"Me neither. I only heard the screaming stop on the inside."

This guy knows how to really hold you now. Maybe you've taught him, but it's probably natural. Love, you have recently learned, cannot be taught.

"Lay down," he says. "Do the memories still come back a lot? Is that what happened?"

"Not often, but that's what happened this time."

"What makes them go away, what brings you back?"

"You do."

He is raising your white T-shirt, kissing at you below. "And before me, what made them go away?"

"Nothing ever did."

"You mean sometimes you never came back?"

"Never in one piece."

Your nipples tickle as he kisses them slowly. "You mean that I sort of brought you back?"

"Yes."

You try and take off his clothes, but he refuses. He unzips your pants, letting your hard dick loose.

Then he takes the yellow tie and gently raises your head, putting the tie around your neck. The soft silk makes you want his tongue all over you. "I guess I can always build another scarecrow," he says, staring at you, his work-in-progress.

Tonight starts off with a gentle tasting, but soon he is feasting all over you, focusing on what is stiffened between your legs. You reach under his shirt and feel his chest hair. Perfection. He chokes a little, then continues sucking as you push your hips closer to him. You want to see his body. With the tie around your neck, he presses just below your bellybutton, milking you like an animal that you never realized you were.

When he rises from you, there is a tiny stream of white running down his bottom lip. He licks it and begins to undress. "Do you want me?"

"Yes."

"When I suck you," he says, "I forget all about the scarecrow..." He is naked now, his dick sliding up and down your chest. "Make me forget again."

You take the tie from your neck and place it around his.

As he leans forward, you take him fiercely and loyally, hoping that he will be able to forget today's earlier event forever. You look up at him as his shaft paints your tongue. With the yellow tie around his neck, and his flat stomach at your eyes, you feel yourself growing hard again. His low, soft moans become the music of the moment. He comes and you swallow hard, getting all of it.

That night, you take turns holding each other. Neither one of you wears the tie. Instead you both hold onto an end of it, making sure you are both still there when the new week begins.

35

"The whole town looks different to me now," you tell the doctor, who always listens even when you think that he's not. No matter how many times he changes the brightness of the lamp on his desk, he give you his full attention.

"What do you mean?"

You left work early to come here and feel all sweaty. It's a carpenter's smell that only they and those they love ever really sense. You still feel that the doctors can smell the sawdust from your skin and the smell of nails that come from your shirt. You are thinking too much about this, thinking of how you should have left work earlier just for a shower. Preoccupied.

"How does the town look to you? Gary?" Hearing him say your name, is all that you need to stop thinking about the house that you spent all day working on.

"It seems like I'm on the outside looking in."

"You've told me that before."

"But this time it's different."

"How so?" He turns the light a little lower. You are so used to him doing this. One of these days you'll ask him why.

"Because I kind of like it. Before, I felt like I didn't belong. Now I feel like I don't belong, but I'm glad that I don't. I don't want to be part of anything around here."

"Anything?"

"Anything." You say this in a way that is so strong you know that he can't follow it up. Case closed.

"Have you been hearing the voices?"

"They were real. They stopped, but I found out where they came from. A young man had a jam box, and he was blasting opera from the field. But he got busted and fined."

"What happened to him?"

The office is just cool enough now. Sweat dries on carpenters the way paint dries on artists. "He sort of lives with me now."

"I see. So no more blackouts or noises?"

"Only once. But I stayed pretty much under control, thanks to him. I heard soldiers coming, I could actually hear their boots on the soft grass. And I was inside the trailer. Then reality kicked back in."

"What kind of relationship do you have?"

"We are in love."

He seems surprised. "Changes," he says.

"Yes, you should see him. He's all lanky and smart and quotes poetry as though he's simply reciting the alphabet."

"Does your ex-wife know?"

"Everybody knows. I bet you even know. The town's that small. When we go to the Piggly Wiggly or anywhere, people stare."

"Are you sure it's you two that they're looking at?"

"I am."

He shifts in his chair. You wonder what he is writing on your file. One of these days, you'll steal it. "How?"

"They call us names, they spray-paint our trailer with the words like 'queer.'"

"This staring doesn't bother you? These words?"

"They used to. Until I saw the way that he strides with this dog tag against his white shirt, through any place in town and blocks it all out. It's like he marks his own spot. Wherever he is, is just as much his as anyone else's. He looks like we did back in the war, terrified, always surrounded by the enemy, but he keeps going."

"That's why you love him?" He turns the light up again.

"I don't know. I think I love him because I don't know how not to love him. Does that make sense?" you ask, as if he's going to say no. "But he is a little strange at times. Like when he said the scarecrow disappeared. I don't know what he did with it. I don't know why he lied."

"You look well, Gary. But still as thin as ever. I wonder who the scarecrow is now. You or this boy you are talking about."

"He looks like you and me. Back when we were beautiful young men."

"We still are," he reminds you. You look at the clock, the fifty minutes are nearly up. "How's your medication?"

"Fine."

"The dosages are okay?"

"I don't need them," you tell him.

"I'd better write you out some, just in case you do."

It is then that you see in his eyes what you, so recently, usually had in yours. The glassiness of his beautiful eyes is riveting and unsettling. Sky-high. Takes one to know one. Dealers in white coats. Their street corner is an office desk, all legal, all the same as the guy that Zachary used to buy from.

You don't stop him from writing out the scrips. He lowers the light, then turns it back up all in a matter of seconds. "Doctor, can you tell me one thing? Why do you always change the power of the light when I'm sitting here?"

"I do it to everyone."

"Why?"

"Because I don't know how not to."

"And all this time, I thought it was me."

He shakes his head. "It's like the love you described, when you can't help yourself."

"I guess the war affected us all in our own way."

"You bet. Sometimes, I see a surgery light when I look at this and sometimes I see a desk lamp. But I know how to control it." By the highness of his tilted head you are sure that he does.

"Doctor," you say, on the way out. "Do you think

that the scarecrow really did disappear?"

"No," he says.

"Good. Because I thought that I was losing my mind."

"But I wouldn't mention it to anyone else," he says. You will not.

You take the prescriptions from him, because it seems to make him happy. But on your way to the door, you begin to tear them up because you don't know how not to. You've learned not to take them, and you don't want to get rid of all of the birds in Petulia. Like so many other things, you don't know how not to.

36

When you return from the doctor, he is in the field building a new creation. A scarecrow, but one less like the others. You stare at the trailer with the hate written all over it, wondering what color you'll paint over it. Or if you'll even paint it at all. You wave at him from the window. The field has begun to grow tall with weeds. It is time to cut it down, you know. But you've been too tired lately. Overworked. But you dread each day of carpentry less, knowing that you have him to come home to.

It is nice to have someone to order pizza with and dance around barefoot in the kitchen with. These are the things that keep you going. They make you forget all about the stares you get around town. At work people are mostly silent about the town gossip. But Richard did come up to you, just two days ago, and simply say, "It's all right by me." It felt good to hear that. Another ally.

On this night, you listen to Carole King's *Tapestry* album as though you've never heard it before. Zachary was only a year old when the album came out and loves it more than you. He seems to think it is the album of his generation and not yours. You listen to it as you try to fall asleep, wondering if, by the end of it, you'll be lulled into a deep, slow fuck.

But tonight he is talking a lot. About his birthday, which is tomorrow. He complains about being twenty-seven so soon. "Double that," you tell him, "then freak out."

He goes to the kitchen and returns with an apple, which he eats with his crooked sharp teeth. "I remember carrying that Carole King album with me everywhere I went," he says. "It's traveled with me since I was sixteen."

He's pretty much moved in here now, rarely staying at his mother's. You're unable to imagine it any other way. Even trying to remember what life was like before him is a series of quick flashes. You remember Gina and her somber housekeeping, Lula holed up in her room. All of that seems centuries ago.

"Remember when I told you that I wanted to be a poster but was never beautiful enough to be one," he says. "When I'm with you, I feel like a poster. It doesn't even matter that much."

"You still don't even know what you look like, do you?"

"Do you?"

"Sometimes."

"Sometimes, too. Would you recognize you if you saw yourself on the street?"

"No, well, maybe, but it might take a while."

"Why does being a poster mean so much to you?"

"It doesn't have to be a poster. It could be a really cool painting. Just to be immortalized. It could even be tacky, as long as it exists."

You refuse to tell him he's beautiful again, because it's like talking to a stone wall. Like you, he won't believe words that come from people that love him.

"But it doesn't matter anymore. I feel okay enough with you and that makes me feel okay with me."

"Good," you smile, both of you growing drowsy.

These nights are filled with oversized images and sounds you don't tell him about. Your dreams contain things that don't belong together, unsynchronized in a disturbing way. Things like Jimi Hendrix and opera music, boots crashing down on your face. A stampede. You feel yourself being walked over, unable to breathe or join the battle. Flashing back. Again.

When you awake from terror this night, you sit up, wet from the sweat that the unreality has drenched you with. You breathe hard but try to control it like last night and the night before so you won't wake him. But tonight he rises, a hand on your left arm.

"It's okay," he says, "you're just having dreams again. None of it is real."

"Will it ever stop?"

"Yes," he assures you, pulling you on top of him, holding you. "Yes. It will stop."

And you don't know why, but you believe him. His body remains still enough to calm you, the way he starts the Carole King record over, the way he gets up and brings you a glass of water. These are things that make you believe he knows what he is talking about. It makes you want to take a picture of him. Especially when he comes from the kitchen with yet another apple, all of the room's reflected light in the window attaching itself to him. A poster.

At nineteen, when some of his peers were already in their second year of college, Zachary found himself at Covenant House on Sunset Boulevard. It was like a jail where they let the kids out during the day to work the streets, while all along telling them not to, and then everyone would report back around six.

Zachary wanted to be like the others, destitute, with no home to go back to. But he simply couldn't say "I am gay" to them, so it was like he didn't have a family at all. He had gone to Los Angeles to be a screenwriting demon who would tear the town up instead of it tearing him down.

It was a long way from Petulia, where he would sit in his darkened room, the windows open, listening to Romancing the Oldies, *loving it when they played "It Never Rains in California." He'd sat in that darkened room for months, writing and dreaming of things that he later realized were fantasies. Carole King kept him grounded to a certain extent; but as the trucks rolled by on the freeway, he believed that a house in Malibu was where he belonged.*

Instead of that house on that beach, he was here among

drug addicts and desperate drag queens. "I won't be happy until I have twelve thousand dollars," one of them told him. When Zachary asked why, the guy explained that a sex change was the only way he could go on living.

Each night, everyone at Covenant House had a different roommate. And each night, most of the guys fucked each other. Zachary never did, because he didn't want to die before he got the house in Malibu.

One night, he roomed with a German guy who took a shower, then proceeded to walk around in a towel saying, "I love Bowie. Bowie is God," then turned to Zachary and said, "You look like Bowie." Zachary was quiet and went to sleep.

During the day, Zachary job-hunted. The people at the House would give him two bus passes per day. And because he had no sense of direction, he would always end up lost without much money. And sometimes, in certain areas, men would roll down their window and ask if he was lost. Once when he was looking for a street called Curson, and a man who smelled really expensive and drove one of those cars that Zachary associated with power stopped, he got in. "What's the address you're looking for?"

Zachary fumbled around for the restaurant address where he was applying for a job. "I can't find it."

"Just calm down. It's California. Everything is going to be all right..." The man spoke with an accent, but Zachary wasn't sure exactly where he came from. His voice was like Mike Brady on Ecstasy.

Then they looked at each other, and in this handsome man's eyes, he felt his neck snap a little and swallowing become a forced activity.

"Stop here," Zachary was led to say.

"But why don't you come over to my house and we can look for the address in the phone book."

"Please stop," Zachary said as politely as he had ever said anything.

The man stopped the car. "Good luck," he said. "Really. Good luck."

Later that night, his roommate was a beautiful glam-rocker who had supposedly fucked a girl from a famous punk band. His name was Jamie and after smoking some pot, he kept Zachary awake by talking. "Those blisters on your feet," said Jamie. "I can put something on them."

"Okay."

Five minutes later they were kissing and it felt like he had come to California just to get that kiss. "Would you fuck me if I had a condom?" Jamie wondered.

"I don't know. Do you have one?"

"No. But we can jerk each other off."

"Is that safe?"

"Yes, my ex-lover, this dancer, he's got it, but I'm okay. Anyway, I'm going to live forever." Jamie raised Zachary's shirt. "Come on. Let's jerk off."

And they did. Zachary showered as soon as the come hit the sheets.

When Zachary was sure Jamie was sleeping, he packed all of his things. He felt terrified of what had just taken place and knew that he had to leave that room, leave the scene. He knew that he was being sucked into a world that would not only never lead to a house in Malibu, but a house anywhere.

He walked across the street to the office. "I want to go home," he told the red-haired woman on duty. "I am not ready to die." He wanted to cry, but those tears stayed in and spread around the insides of him, mixing with his blood, making him unable to speak clearly.

"Do you have a family to go back to?"

"Yes," he finally spoke. "They are wonderful."

"Then what are you doing here?"

He stared at the street where he thought he'd be strong enough to make a living. But now he felt like a coward, unable to fuck rich men, unable to steal or just get high and play in the streets all day.

"Why are you here?" she asked again.

"I...you know..."

"Just say it," she told him. "It's okay. Just say it..."

And not even to her at that moment, even though they both knew, could he tell her that he was what many people back in Petulia had always accused him of being. Finally he said, "I am what those people back home said I am."

"Good. Now let's call your mother..."

"I'm nineteen years old. Don't call her. Just get me a ticket home."

The lady made him call his mom, who was just glad he was coming back home. Since his plane wasn't leaving until that night, he wandered the streets, hoping that someday he could return and have his own secure place in the California sun. He walked along Sunset Boulevard, and with the four dollars he had left, he bought a pair of cheap Wayfarers. Waiting until it was time to go to the airport turned into the longest day he'd ever experienced. But he felt good to be free even if he was going back to a place where he didn't belong

At one point, with his Wayfarers on, his walk turned into a run and he ran a few blocks, his head and body attached firmly, his breathing just like it was supposed to be. He looked up a few times to see that the sky was blue enough to soar through without a plane. Though he knew it wasn't possible, he thought about what a wonderful thing it would be to have the sky open up and swallow him whole.

37

Gina has called. Her voice seems much softer than the last times she's called. There's almost a confused sound to her voice, like she's not sure that she's called the right person. She wants to come over and talk about Lula. She says she's worried about her. "She's fine," you tell her, not knowing why Gina or you should believe each other about anything at this point. You are both liars. Masters.

You want to tell her that you've heard voices, that you've woken up sweating, but you refrain. Holding back information from the one person who knows you best is like having your voice box cut out.

"I'll cook," you say.

"Will he be there?"

"Yes. It's his birthday."

You sense her reluctance, but she surprises you. "Okay, I'll come. I think we ought to talk about Lula. I've been reading books, and they say that if a person's father is...you know...then...well, we'll talk about it when I get there."

You hang up, feeling calm, knowing that the worst scenes with Gina are over. You are too weary to fight with her, and you know she is too. Or else one would have just occurred on the phone. Double surrender flags. This war with no sturdy sides to it, can't be won.

You almost want to see her. Time has passed. Enough to allow you to relax and accept what your doctor called "the moment" the other day. Zachary, you, contentment.

As Zachary hangs out in the field rebuilding a new scarecrow, you stay in and watch the Saints on a roll, beating the Atlanta Falcons. You're barbecuing in the oven. But when you smell smoke, you look outside to see him as he sets the remains of the old scarecrow on fire.

Cremation. You rush to the door, worrying that he is setting the whole field on fire. He's told you the stories of his fire-starting youth, but he takes a fire extinguisher and puts it out. Then he begins working on the newer one he's almost finished with.

You look at the outside of the graffitied trailer. You've grown accustomed to people yelling from their trucks, honking their horns. They don't bother you. None of this can compare to a dark night in an Asian jungle. Here, you have more hope than when you were over there.

You yell a little when the Falcons intercept the football. But you don't do it too loud, so that you don't alarm Zachary. You don't freak out about it. And while you don't tell him, because it's been in your control, you have heard some things that you know don't exist. You've heard the boots again, as clearly as if you were marching in the platoon. One morning not long ago, you woke to the sound of a helicopter, but when you went to the window there was nothing there but birds in their morning flight. They seemed rowdy, like a group of flying teenagers coming down from a night of clubbing.

When Gina arrives, you don't know what to expect; you are actually relaxed. Control takes over. She knocks this time before entering, and you yell for her to come in. The Saints are losing now. This was to be expected. You're yelling at the television set. "Come in," you say loudly to her.

She looks a little somber, holding a dark-chocolate birthday cake. "Is everything all right?" you ask her.

"Yes, I just thought that the bakery would close before I got there." Nothing's changed except her expression. There is almost a smile on her face, but it seems forced. You remember when it was natural, but you've learned that memories are not necessarily good for you. You look to see that Zachary is still in the field reading. He is like that, recognizing a moment for what it is. Space. That's one of the reasons you love him.

"You look great," you say, not wanting to tell her that worry has fully bloomed on her face. She is shaking to the point where it seems as though the cake is like a ton of bricks.

"I must say," she states, "you look healthy, Gary. You look really healthy."

You take the cake from her and place it on the table. "Are we going to fight now?" you ask, turning off the ball game.

"No," she says, "no fighting. But I do have to say that's the first time you ever turned off the football game while I was in the room." She is walking around the trailer with an apprehension you don't understand.

You can't deny that turning off a ball game is a big deal for you. She joins you at the kitchen table. "It's good to see you're well," you say, wondering how long you can keep this up. Basically what you are thinking is that you are over all of this.

"Something smells good."

"I'm barbecuing in the oven. After somebody took the grill."

"I took things I didn't need," she says. "I hated you then."

"I know. I was hateable."

"He's out in the field, isn't he?" She motions toward the window. "He seems real creative. An artist-type."

"That's what he went to school for. He's a good guy."

"Good."

"How's Eddie?" You ask this and feel your heart sink. It's the polite question. Marching boots move around the outside of your ear. With her around, you feel as though you must really ignore these sounds.

"He's good, just got a promotion. He's running for sheriff, you know."

"Good luck," you think, then lie yet again. You're

not totally over these white niceties. "Good for him."

"It made me feel good to buy that birthday cake." She almost seems embarrassed. You touch her face.

"Thank you." Then you see tears in her eyes, but nothing seeps out.

"Don't cry on me, Gina. You seem so happy, what's wrong? Wanna drink?"

"Bourbon."

"It's only Coca-Cola and orange juice."

"Juice." She seems stunned.

You want her to get up and get it herself. Even though she's cleaned you out, your home still feels like she belongs there. The orange juice seems to make her drunk. Her words slur. Sweet emotion, LSU, shared personal histories.

"In the beginning, it didn't matter." She wipes the orange juice from her mouth, like it's whiskey. "But each time I passed, and I saw the letters painted on the trailer, the house that used to be ours, I felt like it had been done not only you, but to me and that young man, Zachary."

"You didn't paint those words." A helicopter approaches. A bomb is dropping; you wait for the next and dive under the table. You didn't want her to see this. But she doesn't do anything, except keep talking.

"And then, when I'd be in town or working at the Tastee-Freez, people would look at me, the way I used to look at people who are like you, and I knew they were seeing what they thought I was. And I knew that you must have spent all these years feeling them looking at you, the way they looked at me."

You are shaking, the entire trailer is shaking.

"You didn't paint those words." Your voice is cracking. You hear footsteps.

"Yes, I did." Her revelation makes her face look pale.

"They are coming," you say.

"I don't hate you anymore," she says. "I love Eddie, but I don't hate you. It would have been nice if it had all worked out like we planned." She's talking to you, but it's as though she's saying it to an invisible person in front of her. Talking to the air.

"They are coming," you repeat. From beneath the table you feel for the dog tags you don't have. How will they identify you when they find you on the ground?

"Do you have a cutting knife for the cake, or did I take that, too?" She is wandering around the kitchen, opening and closing every door.

You are wearing bright colors, you'll be obvious. And then the sirens grow louder, the bombs ring out, consecutively deafening you. They have arrived. Shelter. Zachary.

You leave her wielding the knife, hovering above the cakeless table. You rush for the front door, tripping soberly down the steps, and rush across the front yard. In his white T-shirt he smiles at you and waves.

You turn for the briefest moment to look at the trailer and see Gina's motionless silhouette glued to the window. Now you run toward him. The cop car moves slowly by. And as your birthday boy with his wondrously crooked body and grin waves anxiously, the shots ring out. Two. Drive-by.

Zachary becomes red. As the car picks up speed, you see the future sheriff gaze from the front seat, but you don't let his eyes go any further into you. As you run across the highway, the car speeds away. Zachary will live. You know this, because you hear the music, and the scarecrow is still in one piece. Complete.

38

He is red and bleeding and making sounds that you haven't heard in years, but always knew would come again. His dog tags reveal his name, and as you reach down and breathe your shallow breaths into his mouth that has kissed you so solemnly, you hope that it is all a mistake and that the dog tags actually have another name on them.

This time, when the choppers and the bullets grow quieter, they are not simply silenced, they are moving backward, finding their place in a history book where they belong. Encyclopedia, volume V.

Pumping on his chest is like you're just grabbing at his ribs. You are becoming as red as he is. And you can't breathe anymore. You don't wonder where your platoon is. They are also in the pages of a book they should have been in all your life. But now you need them most. Each breath you put into him is not only an exhaustive attempt to revive him, but a screaming of "help."

Then he looks at you, his eyes finally open. He can see again. You knew it could happen, even with your fingers clutching his insides as though holding onto them is like plugging yourself into him. "Zachary," you say.

"I never was asleep on the grass like this before," he gurgles in that way that only those who are saying good-bye to a lover can. You know that if he could laugh he would, if only slightly. He is bleeding in colors that you are seeing for the first time, and since you have no ladle you try and throw some blood, which is mixed with grass and weeds, back into him. You know life doesn't work this way, but right now it seems like it might.

In the distance, you remember the music but you don't actually hear it. You raise his limp left hand to your face. "You didn't shave," he says, leaving you with nothing to do but smile. His hands feel as soft as the first time he touched you and now you remember when it was. You remember how he picked you off the floor of that bar and held your hand as he put you in his bed. It's not coming back in flashbacks either. It's coming back in a full scene. The way his cologne smelled, the fact that he was the one, begging his friends to stay for one more song. You know that these are the kinds of hands only certain people have, soft and full of energy, even when the life has been dripping out of them. War-wounds. Silence.

Then he begins to speak in that language he used weeks ago on the same grass. It is English but it is intoxicating. It is like another language to you. Maybe it's the way he's saying it; maybe it's just the· fact that he's speaking at all that makes it all so foreign. "This is the way the world ends," he whispers. The harder you press his hand to the tears on your cheeks, the more you learn his language. "This is the way the world ends," he repeats. You don't even question if he knows what he's saying; you're sure it means something that only people who read books, like him, fully understand.

What's left of him is in your arms now. He is light, but his words make him heavy, make him still alive. He is skin and bones. Suddenly his turning physically into much of nothing, has turned him into everything. Then he says it again. "This is the way the world ends." You are standing now. You know that if you can get him to a hospital, doctors can take him from you and stuff all the essentials back into him and put him back together again.

You hold him, which is like holding not only his life but your own in your very arms. "Not with a bang," he says roughly, his hand sliding from your face to his own cheek, "but a whimper."

Then you feel yourself drop him. Your arms free of

the minimal weight that you immediately want back. When you look on the ground, you don't see him. But in front of you, there he is, hovering like a bird in one of his favorite paintings. And you reach out at first, but something about his closed eyes, your remembrance of boots against boots, a skinny boy in a faded room, a moon-shaped bar of soap, all hold you back.

You watch him rise, his multicolored blood, all of his missing chest, swarming up like a fountain pen exploding in reverse, the ink finding its way back to where it belongs. Home.

And finally, you see him in one piece again. Beautiful. Again you stop yourself from reaching out to him. And you simply watch him rise up carrying all of himself away. But somewhere you see him begin to break into pieces. This time, however, they are whole parts, and they soar. First his head, then a left arm and a right leg become detached. They all fly off in different directions. Parts of him spread out across the night. He is everywhere. He is the sky.

You fall to the ground, no tears or sadness hanging in your throat as you sit calmly. There is nothing like watching your lover turn into a dozen birds in various brilliant colors. You watch the man you held and loved like you've never even loved yourself fly out of sight.

Looking down, you see the blood that he has left behind. You and the ground are completely red. Your life has left you. You wonder if someday they'll discover a new species of bird that can talk and sing and quote things from a book in a way that only that certain species can. Your species. You.

39

Gina is inside, stabbing at the window with the butcher knife. You know how cheap the trailer is, how the panes could crack at any moment. You wonder if she is trying to kill the scene she has just witnessed from the window.

You walk inside, wearing Zachary's blood, waiting for her to say something. To take a towel and wipe you clean. To do something besides stand there and look like the drunk you once were. The bizarre array of expressions that you noticed seeping from her face earlier have now become an unremovable mask.

You don't speak. You feel that the bloody footprints you are making on the carpet and the blood on the door handle speak for themselves. You don't know what you are supposed to say to a person who's seen something that must've looked like a bloodbath, but to you was a colorful birth. So you just look at her as she trembles with the knife, twitching the way Zachary used to when he did too much coke.

You walk closer to her, wanting to say something to her, wanting to know what Zachary's rising looked like from inside the creaking trailer.

You listen for the helicopters, knowing that they were there the last time you were in the house. You wonder if you'll have to jump beneath the table with her, protecting yourself and her. It's a good think she's got the knife. You wonder which weapon you'll use. You listen for the enemy that seems to have grown silent. That's when you realize you may never need another weapon again.

She sits on the cedar chest where fish once swam in the tank that she took to Eddie's. She is still holding the knife tightly. She is holding it in that way that lets you know she wants to cut something extremely badly. She seems to be preparing for battle. Her eyes are sharp, wide-open, and glassy blue.

The trailer is quiet now. There is no Carole King, no rambling Zachary, no yelling Gina. There is only a shaki-ness coming from her, a nervousness which rocks the trailer slowly but doesn't scare you. Your enemy now is a silence that you are sure you can defeat. Gina has a look about her now: her eyes remain wide, her face is twisted, half-smiling and yet unhappy.

The night has become dark, and so has her face. She stares at you as if you are the one who has just pulled the trigger. At first you think she's going to come after you with the knife. But after living with someone for more than twenty years, you know if they are a stabber or not. You do not recognize this tangled look on her face, as she ages before you, becoming a woman who is not the one you left when you went out into the field. Her eyes spin around the room. She looks stunned. Shell-shocked.

When she stands up and goes to the kitchen, she is muttering something to herself and when you ask her to repeat it, she simply says, "Candles." And she lights them all. "Where's the birthday boy?" she asks.

And for the first time you realize that what she's seen has taken root in every part of her body except her brain. What she has witnessed is written all over her body, and yet she doesn't seem to remember it.

"Do you want some of this cake?" She blows out all of the candles.

For a brief moment, it is like a chunk of your life with her from months ago. You walk over to her and gently shake her by the shoulders, trying to bring her back to your reality. The chocolate cake in her hands simply hangs there before it crashes to the ground. You don't know what to say to a person whose eyes have turned to marbles, whose face has begun to show more wrinkles with each passing moment.

You are thinking of Zachary now and where he'll

wind up, wondering which park or meadow he'll touch down in, to scoop up the bread people throw at him. Maybe you'll have to build a birdhouse.

Gina takes your hand and moves close into you. Her breath on your bloody neck lets you know that she is expecting more. For the first time in ages, you see the need in her and only a few months ago, you would have felt too guilty to refuse. "Please?" she says softly.

"Please," you say, just as softly, but not wanting to lead her on. "Don't do this."

By looking around the silence and the blood, your history together rushes all around you two. The blood-stains of Zachary have taken their places around the house. You can't help but notice that he is gone and still everywhere.

You feel like you're cheating on both of them at the same time, with both of them aware of it. She lets go of you, and you fall to the mattress on the floor. Zachary on the same mattress, in the field, exposed you to who you are. You could share a space with Gina who sits down beside you. You could go through the motions. But living together would never actually be living together. It would just be staying together.

"Gina?" you finally say from the mattress. "He's gone." You are trying to tell her that he died without dying, but don't know how. She looks at you, and it's more apparent now than ever that she honestly cannot acknowledge what she saw from the window earlier. "Gina?"

"Do you think Eddie is such a bad person?"

"Yes." You don't know how else to answer, what else to say to convince her. "He killed Zachary. Didn't you see him? Maybe I should drive you home," you tell her.

"No," she says, drunkenly; maybe it's from the smell of the blood. "I'm fine." You walk her to the door and watch as she stumbles to her car, making sure that she doesn't make some wild decision to run off into the field like you would have months ago.

After you hear the car door slam, you see that she has carved something into the living room wall. It is nothing but your name, in scratchy letters. Gary.

After she's gone, and you're standing alone in the box that is the trailer, everything you touch turns red. You realize what it is like to be alone again, without any army opposing you. The helicopters don't come, the marching has disappeared. You wait to hear her pull away and when you don't, you go outside to the front yard where you find her, trying to start the car, moving in slow motion like she has been all night.

"No," she says again, not looking anywhere near you.

40

That night, after Gina leaves, you lie restless, thinking about pills, but then let the thought go. There is still so much of him in the house. Old shirts, records, necklaces. Things that would be nothing if they had not been Zachary's. It is late when you finally fall asleep. You have no intention of working tomorrow or maybe not even the next day.

By 3 a.m. you're finally able to rest on the scratchy mattress. The sheets remind you way too much of him and how he looked against them. And in your rest, you are awakened by the sounds of feet, not booted this time, but bare, outside, crunching the grass. There is an army, but this time you lie there; you don't sweat or shake; instead you get up out of your shallow sleep and you see them. In the field, they are marching. There must be a thousand complete men in that field. Men like you and Zachary. And while at first they are almost shadowy figures, they become clearer the longer you look. Some of them are skinnier than Zachary, some of them are covered in sores. Some look completely healthy, but walk across the green moonlit grass with their arms in casts, their eyes blackened. Some of them are dressed like women, their makeup perfectly applied, and some of them just look like college frat boys, computer nerds, hippies, and junkies.

The way they march is so much more eloquent than the way you did in boot camp. There is nobody yelling at the soldiers. And they are all totally silent, marching in sync, as if it's not even necessary to speak to each other to keep in step. They don't carry guns or signs, only heads held high. You know that if they had been there when Eddie drove by, Zachary would have been protected. You watch them, guided by the moon, until you fall asleep again.

Lula's on the phone at 7 a.m. You don't want to tell her too much about all the events just yet. "How's Organic?" you ask.

"Good. Daddy, I'm managing the bar now, and Organic's working on cars. We're doing real well. Got a bigger apartment just off St. Charles. We've got a spare room for you to visit."

"Good, Lula."

"What?"

"I'd like to come visit."

"Really, Daddy?" You can't tell if she's happy or surprised. "I'd love to have you here. Plese, please come visit."

"I am going to."

She lets out a scream of joy so loud that you have to move the phone away from your ear. "Daddy, let me just ask you this. Are you ever leaving Petulia?"

"I suppose, maybe someday, Lula."

"Thank God. How's Mom?"

"She's real good, Lula."

"Daddy, come soon. Call me if you get lost and to make sure one of us will be here."

"Thank you, Lula."

"Thank you, Daddy," she says, though you can't imagine for what.

41

Three months after the funeral where they thought they put him in the ground, you still know that he is somewhere else. You've begun to feel settled in New Orleans. You've found an apartment on Decatur. Thanks to Lula, the once overweight mouse, introducing you to all of her friends, you have a lot of steady carpentry work. You no longer build houses or restaurants. You simply fix what's already broken in them.

Most mornings you get up early, go to the Riverwalk, which is so relaxing in the morning that nobody must ever feel out of place here. With its steamboats in the distance and French coffee shops, you feel like a foreigner in a strange land that was always meant to be your home.

Sometimes Lula and you have beignets and coffee on one of the benches and watch the day start.

"Daddy, I'm so glad you got out of Petulia," Lula tells you almost every one of the mornings she joins you. She still doesn't know all of the details of that murderous night. And you don't really want her to have to know them. However, with Gina in the Mandeville State Hospital across the lake, you know it'll all eventually come out.

"I can't believe he did it," Lula says of Eddie the night she helps you move in. "Just dumped her like that. Why?"

"He wants to be sheriff," you remind her.

Sometimes you go visit Gina. Eddie throwing her out took the final toll on a life of paying dues. She refused the trailer at first, but soon after, moved back in and decided to die. She set the trailer on fire and remained inside, running from the firefighters when they tried to rescue her.

She now looks nothing like she did that night when she wanted so desperately to cut Zachary's cake. There is a dazed look about her now. You're sure she's on all sorts of medication. You ask her and she can't even remember half of the names. There are circles under her eyes and streaks of gray highlighting her hair. She still doesn't look her age. For the first time, she looks older.

She doesn't really talk much now. When you visit, you sit at these little round tables with somebody always begging for a cigarette. Gina doesn't beg, but she has taken up smoking. You and Lula make sure she has what she needs. When she does talk, it's mostly at you, but about herself. "You know what I really wanted to do," she says one Monday afternoon. "I really wanted to cut my head off, but I couldn't figure out how to do it correctly."

Now when you think about her, it's of an image of her walking the halls of that mental ward, knowing someday she'll find the strength to get out. You should probably feel guilty for all of this, but you know you're not the only one to blame. Everyone is. "How's your love life?" she always druggedly asks.

"Fine" is all you ever say, wondering if it's saying too much.

There's certainly no need to tell her that you go to the bars once in a while, and that it's still too soon to find somebody else. After all, not everyone can fly away, not everyone can touch your face and re-teach you your native language like Zachary could. So you've stopped looking for him, knowing that someday love may be able to be yours again. But for the first time, this loneliness is almost as good as life with Zachary. And because of him, you learned that it is okay to be alone.

All of this is information that you keep from Gina. Yet unlike before, it is right to hold out and not tell her everything. You know this because you don't feel it boiling, nothing's bottled up. You get out what you need to, through Lula and Organic, and in certain ways, no matter how refrained it seems at times, though Gina.

One weekend, after she's doing better, she gets a weekend pass. She stays with Lula and Organic and, beside seeming sad, she does all right and is supposedly talking more. On Sunday, you are sitting with her and Lula on the bench that has become as familiar as your own apartment. It's one of those mornings when New Orleans is actually cold. It's just above forty degrees and being by the water is really asking for it. "I'm freezing," Lula says. "I've got to go."

"All right," you tell her. She's put on a little weight this winter, but she still looks radiant and clean. A slight smile, not unlike Gina's of days long ago, is almost a permanent expression on her face these days.

You are bundled in a layer of flannel and a heavy wool coat with the inside ripped a bit too much. "I'm going to get you a new jacket, Daddy," she says.

Suddenly Gina laughs. "You've had that thing forever, Gary."

"I know. Christmas, 1977."

"'78," she says. You and Lula look at each other, surprised.

"This one's fine." You say this as you begin to throw the remains of your beignets at the birds, which have come to expect it from you.

"Daddy," Lula says, finally standing up, pinkish from the cold. "You and Mama come by before you drive back to Mandeville." She reaches down and kisses her mother. It's not Lula that surprises you by doing this. It's the tightness with which Gina holds Lula. You can see her draining all of her energy in this hug. Lula puts her black purse around her shoulder. "You two should get out of this cold soon. You'll freeze to death."

"Not us," Gina speaks. "Not us, right, Gary?"

"Right," you say.

After Lula is gone, Gina turns to you. "I do feel better, Gary. You're my good friend." She takes your hand. "You always were."

"You know you're going to be just fine," you tell her.

"I know that. I mean, look at you," she says. "Gary, I know that you don't like women the way I used to think that you did. But do you think I can be beautiful again?"

"Yes," you say. And you mean it. After all, you've seen people in worse shape come back to life.

"How's your love life?" she asks as usual.

"There is no love life," you tell her.

"It may not be me or anybody in particular, but there's always a love life," she says. "Even though I'm bony and old now, I still know there's a love life for me." She lets your hand go. "When I get better, I'm going to fall in love again." She puts her head on your shoulder and asks, "Gary, this isn't the end of our lives, is it?"

"Jesus!" you exclaim. "Gina, this is such a beginning."

She seems to believe you, and she should because it is the ultimate truth. You're glad because the idea of her roaming the halls of a gray state mental ward should not be the end for her. She is smiling now, and not that crazy drugged-out smile you've been seeing so much of. The old one, like the one Lula has now. Even with the grayness and the shivering and the ragged eyes, she has, for the moment, become almost pretty again.

You throw some more of your French donuts to the birds.

"Gary, why aren't you eating that? Lula tells me you do this everyday. Why do you come out here each morning to feed these birds?"

"Because," you tell her as a steamboat whistles in the cold, "they need to be fed."

A native of Louisiana, **Martin Hyatt** holds an MFA in Creative Writing from The New School University. He is the recipient of The New School Chapbook Award for Fiction, and an Edward F. Albee Writing Fellowship. His work has appeared in such publications as *Sandbox* and *Blithe House Quarterly*. He has taught writing and literature at various colleges throughout the New York City area. He currently teaches creative writing and world literature at St. Francis College. He lives in New York City and is working on a new novel.